THE HERO SHE WANTS

UNBROKEN HEROES
BOOK 2

ANNA HACKETT

The Hero She Wants

Published by Anna Hackett

Copyright 2024 by Anna Hackett

Cover by Hang Le Designs

Cover image by ADB Imagery

Edits by Tanya Saari

ISBN (ebook): 978-1-923134-04-1

ISBN (paperback): 978-1-923134-05-8

**The Powerbroker - Romantic Book of the Year
(Ruby) winner 2022**

**Heart of Eon - Romantic Book of the Year
(Ruby) winner 2020**

Cyborg - PRISM Award Winner 2019

**Unfathomed and Unmapped - Romantic Book
of the Year (Ruby) finalists 2018**

**Unexplored – Romantic Book of the Year
(Ruby) Novella Winner 2017**

**Return to Dark Earth – One of Library
Journal's Best E-Original Books for 2015 and
two-time SFR Galaxy Awards winner**

At Star's End – One of Library Journal's Best E-Original Romances for 2014

The Phoenix Adventures – SFR Galaxy Award Winner for Most Fun New Series and "Why Isn't This a Movie?" Series

Beneath a Trojan Moon – SFR Galaxy Award Winner and RWAus Ella Award Winner

Hell Squad – SFR Galaxy Award for best Post-Apocalypse for Readers who don't like Post-Apocalypse

"Like Indiana Jones meets Star Wars. A treasure hunt with a steamy romance." – SFF Dragon, review of *Among Galactic Ruins*

"Action, danger, aliens, romance – yup, it's another great book from Anna Hackett!" – Book Gannet Reviews, review of *Hell Squad: Marcus*

Sign up for my VIP mailing list and get your *free box set* containing three action-packed romances.

Visit here to get started: www.annahackett.com

CHAPTER ONE

It was probably wrong how much she liked mud.

Crouching down to examine a shard of pottery, she smiled. Okay, not mud so much—which was currently coating her work boots and the bottom of her cargo pants. What she really liked was what she *uncovered* in the mud.

Archeologist Hayden Sinclair gently worked a piece of pottery free and briefly studied the engravings before setting it on a tray with some others.

She lifted her head and scanned the dig.

She and a multinational team of researchers were working on a site in Nicaragua.

El Cascal de Flor de Pino, near the town of Kukra Hill, predated the Maya, and they'd found evidence of an ancient town and several outlying villages that dated from almost three thousand years ago. The petroglyphs and pottery were remarkable, and it appeared the town was a center for the production of ceremonial columns used at burial sites.

"Why do you look so damn happy?"

The grumpy female voice made her look up. Maria Rodriguez was about fifteen years older than Hayden, and in her mid-forties. The woman was frighteningly competent, and exceptionally good at her job. Her dark hair was in a tidy braid, and her hands were planted firmly on her hips.

Hayden grinned at her friend. "Because uncovering history, especially undiscovered history, is why I became an archeologist. There is so much we can learn."

Maria grunted. "It wouldn't be so bad if there was less mud, and a decent coffee shop nearby."

They were fairly remote out here, and there wasn't a coffee shop in sight. There was a quirky little coffee shop in Kukra Hill, and while the coffee wasn't great, the food was good.

Smiling, Hayden rose. "I agree, but I'm still happy."

Her friend leaned in and lowered her voice. "Your father is trying to contact you. He said you aren't answering your satellite phone."

Hayden felt a spurt of annoyance. Once again, her father managed to make her feel like a teenager, not a twenty-eight-year-old woman. "I'm working."

"He's just checking that you're all right."

"I know you give him updates."

Maria's dark gaze was unwavering. "Because it's my job."

Hayden turned away and ran a hand over her hair. The jungle humidity made it stick to her scalp and the back of her neck. "He wants to lure me back for some political event, and play the happy family. I'm *working*.

He doesn't always respect that. I'm not a pawn to be moved around on a chessboard."

"Hayden, you *are* a happy family."

"I know." She loved her dad, but he still drove her crazy. She sighed. "I'll call him."

"Good."

"Dr. Claire?" One of the Nicaraguan researchers appeared. "Dr. Stephenson's uncovered some new pottery. It might be a burial. He'd like you to take a look."

"Thanks, Pedro."

To everyone here, she was Dr. Haley Claire. Archeologist. Not Hayden Sinclair, daughter of the President of the United States of America.

Maria wasn't really her assistant. She was the highly trained Secret Service agent assigned to protect her.

Her father had wanted her to have a full security detail. Scratch that. He hadn't wanted her to come here at all. He often forgot that she wasn't his subordinate, and that she was an adult. Her mother had died of cancer two years ago. Hayden stood still for a moment, absorbing the piercing grief. She missed her mom something crazy. The grief was an aching wound that had dulled but never went away. Her mother's death had made her father more protective.

Hayden had really wanted to be a part of this dig. She'd argued him down to one Secret Service agent, and that they'd use aliases.

She had no desire to go back to Washington, D.C. Her father had been in politics most of her life. He'd been a businessman beforehand, then he'd seen more than his share of injustices, and he'd wanted to help fix them.

Hayden hated political life. She admired the few politicians who truly wanted to make a difference, but most were sharks—out for power and influence.

She'd navigated those waters since she was a teenager. All the fakeness and insincerity left her feeling ill. All the people who smiled at you, while they lied and manipulated behind your back.

People who betrayed you.

Her belly tightened and she lifted her chin. She shoved the new slash of emotion down deep. This was *her* life. Her dad had to accept that she was doing things her way.

That meant no manipulative men. No drama. Just work.

And the pesky Secret Service agent she loved like a big sister. Maria had been on her detail for over a decade, and while she never forgot Maria had a job to do, it hadn't stopped them from becoming good friends.

"Come on, *Mary*." She used the agent's fake name. "Let's take a look at this new pottery."

The agent groaned but followed. Their boots squelched on the muddy ground.

Hayden glanced at the clouds building on the horizon above the lush green trees that surrounded the dig site. They'd get another storm later in the day. For the moment, the sun was shining, but the humidity was building. Hayden's khaki shirt stuck to her back, and wisps of her shoulder-length blonde hair stuck to her face, no matter what she did.

As they reached Dr. Stephenson's area of the dig, she saw the archeologist waving at her. He was tall, gangly, with a long-boned face that always looked a little bemused.

"He has a crush on you," Maria murmured.

Hayden snorted. "He's two years younger than me."

"So?"

"And somehow he seems ten years younger."

"He is...boyish."

Lewis Stephenson was a geek, who didn't have much to say unless it had to do with pre-Columbian Central American history. But he was kind and worked well with everyone on the team.

"Besides," Hayden shot her friend a look, "I don't want a man."

Maria was silent for a moment. "You have to get over Douchebag Dillon eventually."

Hayden's stomach tightened. "I *am* over him," she said, through clenched teeth.

"No, you're not."

"I have no feelings for that man." Catching your loving fiancé banging his assistant on his desk tended to kill most feelings quickly. "Except for anger."

"You have to let it go, Hay, or it'll fester."

The man who had proclaimed to love her, who had no political ambitions, or interest in her father's office, had wormed his way through her defenses, made her believe what they shared was real.

It had all been a lie.

"I'll always be angry at him. He's a liar and a cheat." The sad fact was, cheating was the least of his crimes. "He wanted access to my father. He was already making deals with damn criminals, convincing them he could influence Dad." The worst bit had been that Dillon had thought she was his ticket to being president himself, one day. Ugh, she hated him.

"You're angry at yourself, but it's not your fault. He fooled us all. Hell, I liked him. He was charming and funny."

Hayden's heart throbbed in the center of her chest. Dillon Driskell was nothing to her. Just an ugly footnote and a hard lesson.

She would never, ever be fooled again.

A dark SUV, splattered in mud, suddenly pulled up on the bumpy, dirt road leading into the dig site. She lifted a hand to shield her eyes. "Who's that? Are we expecting anyone today?"

Maria frowned, gaze zeroing in on the SUV. "There was no one on the approved list."

Five men in khaki pants and shirts got out of the vehicle.

It all happened so fast. One second, they were walking into the dig, the next, they pulled weapons—automatic rifles—and started firing.

Hayden watched workers fall. Her brain couldn't comprehend what she was seeing. Dr. Stephenson waved his arms at the attackers, yelling something.

Lewis' body shook under the impact of bullets.

No. *No.* Horror hit her, freezing her insides.

"Come on." Maria's hand clamped on her wrist. The agent had her gun drawn and was pulling Hayden in the opposite direction.

Her heartbeat thundered in her ears. Around her,

screams mixed with the sound of gunfire. Adrenaline surged into her veins.

"I'm afraid you aren't going anywhere, Ms. Sinclair."

They swiveled. Three more men stood behind them. Two had weapons aimed at Maria.

The man in the middle had swarthy skin, dark stubble on his jaw, and black eyes. He looked Nicaraguan, but his English was perfect with no accent.

Oh, no. He knew who she was. Hayden desperately tried to keep her face blank.

Maria shifted, angling her body in front of Hayden. "You're mistaken, this is Dr. Claire—"

The gunshot was deafening, and Hayden cried out.

She saw the hole in Maria's forehead, a second before the woman's body collapsed to the muddy ground.

"No!" Hayden screamed. She lunged for her friend. "*Maria.*"

But strong arms grabbed her, yanking her off her feet. She struggled wildly as a black hood was dropped over her head.

Maria. God, Maria.

As she was carted away, she kept fighting. Kicking and squirming. But it was no use. More hands grabbed her legs, holding her still. There were too many of them, and they were all too strong.

"No!"

———

HE TURNED the wrench and tried to unfasten the bolt. He gritted his teeth. "Come on, you stubborn little mother—" His hand slipped and he scraped his knuckles. "Fucking hell."

Shepherd "Shep" Barlow straightened from under the hood of the old truck and shook his hand.

"Piece of junk." He kicked the tire. The truck was an old Chevy that he'd had the idea of restoring.

He was currently regretting that choice.

He had a two-year old Dodge Ram that ran just fine. He didn't need this old heap of junk.

The phone in his pocket vibrated, and he stiffened. He pulled his phone out. His perimeter sensor alarms had just been triggered. He tapped the phone screen, muttering as he smeared grease on it.

The video feed showed a car coming up his driveway. It was a black, official-looking sedan, not the usual truck or SUV you most often saw in the Colorado Rockies.

His place was three hours out of Denver. He didn't get many visitors, mainly because he preferred it that way. He rarely invited anybody.

He cleaned his hand on a rag, and watched the black sedan pull up in front of the barn.

This couldn't be good.

The back door opened, and Shep checked the Glock tucked in the back of his jeans. You could take the man out of the military, but it didn't happen the other way around. He was always armed.

The man who got out of the car was in his sixties, and fit for his age. He was wearing a suit. His hair was a lot grayer than the last time Shep had seen him.

Shep strode over. "General Rand. It's been a long time, sir."

"Barlow." The older man looked around. "Nice place you have here."

Shep's piece of land had once been a silver mine during the boom times of the 1800s. There was an old, wooden structure still up on the hill, and the hillside was riddled with tunnels.

More recently, the place had been turned into holiday cabin rentals. The cabins were still in pretty good repair—except for getting shot up recently, when he'd helped out an old military buddy. Shep lived in one cabin, kept another one maintained for guests—which he tried to limit as much as possible. Spending time with people was at the bottom of his priority list.

"How did you find me?" he asked the general.

"Vander Norcross."

Shep straightened. Vander was Shep's old Ghost Ops commander. They'd served together in Delta before they'd been recruited for the government's top-secret special forces program.

They'd done jobs that no one else could do. In places no one else had wanted to go.

Vander was a man Shep trusted with his life, but his old commander had also accused Shep of hiding up on his mountain. And he'd vowed to do something about it.

Shep was fucking fine where he was.

"My little slice of the Rockies," he said. "It's quiet, peaceful." He cocked his head. "I thought you'd retired, General?"

The man gave him a faint smile. "I am retired. Officially."

And unofficially, he probably did something black ops.

Yeah, this couldn't be good.

"Come in." Shep gestured toward his cabin. "I'll make some coffee."

The general followed him inside. The cabin was all gleaming wood, with a decent kitchen Shep had renovated himself, and a large, stone fireplace. In the kitchen, he set the coffee machine going.

Once the machine was finished, Shep poured coffee into two mugs. He handed one to Rand, then leaned a hip against the counter. "Still take it black, I assume?"

"Same as you." The general sipped.

"You want to tell me what you're doing here?"

"I always liked that about you, Shep. Frank, and straight to the point."

Shep snorted. "Got my knuckles rapped a few times for not keeping my mouth shut."

"Not that you cared."

Shep sipped his coffee. "Nope. Still don't."

"We have a situation. A woman's life...and national security, are on the line."

Shep frowned. "Go on."

"Dr. Hayden Sinclair was abducted off an archeological dig in Nicaragua this morning."

Taking another sip of his coffee, Shep wondered why that name sounded vaguely familiar.

"Dr. Sinclair is the president's daughter." The general pulled out a photo from his jacket pocket and put it on the counter.

She was attractive. Blonde hair brushing her shoulders, and large, brown eyes. Her hair was lots of different shades, and reminded him of the homemade caramels he sometimes bought in town. He could tell she was smart. She had that direct look that said she was one step ahead of you. The best thing about her was the strong jaw line that made her face interesting. Not just another blonde, plastic socialite.

Her chin was tilted in the photo, like she was saying a silent *fuck you.*

He met General Rand's gaze. "The President of the United States?"

"That's the one."

"What the fuck was the president's daughter doing in Nicaragua?"

"Working on a dig site."

Shep's eyebrows winged up. "With no security?"

"She had a Secret Service agent with her." The general's mouth flattened. "Agent Rodriguez was shot in the head and killed."

Fuck. "So is the president sending a team in to retrieve her?"

"Things are...delicate with US and Nicaragua relations right now. They have elections coming up. We can't be seen to be interfering. The president can't send a sanctioned team in."

"Bet the president isn't too happy about that." Shep took another sip of coffee.

"No, he's beside himself. She's his only child, and he lost his wife not too long ago. But this goes beyond Ms. Sinclair's well-being."

Shep felt that all-too-familiar prickle at the back of

his neck. The one he always got when shit was about to hit the fan.

The general set his coffee mug down. "We got word that whoever has her is shopping her around. As potential leverage against our country."

Shep shook his head. "Shit."

"If they sell her to a terrorist group, or an unfriendly nation, they could use her against the president."

Shep shook his head. "Sounds like a mess."

"It is. One I need you to fix."

Now Shep froze. "Me? I'm retired."

"I know, but you're one of very few men I know who has the skills to pull this off. Alone."

Shep shook his head. *Fuck, no.*

"Go in and get her out. Quietly. We'll give you whatever support we can, but there has to be no tie to the government—"

"Go in, alone, and if I get caught, you have no knowledge of me."

The general nodded.

"This is a suicide mission." Shep had stopped doing those a long time ago.

The general tapped the photo. "A young woman's life is on the line."

Shep looked down at the picture again. At the tilt of Hayden Sinclair's chin, her half smile. She had soft looking lips.

He cleared his throat. "There are other people—"

"She needs you, Shep. Vander recommended you. You can save her. Vander said you were the right man for this."

Fuck. He was going to punch Vander next time he saw him. "Why?"

"Because you have the skill set. Because you would never leave an innocent woman in enemy hands."

Fucking fuck. He looked at that picture again. Blonde hair, brown eyes, and that stubborn jaw.

"And because one of the groups looking to buy her is a Taliban cell run by Khalid Mohammad Omari."

Cold swept through Shep. The man who had killed three of Shep's Ghost Ops friends. A sadistic monster. Suddenly, there weren't nearly enough fucks to cover this situation.

CHAPTER TWO

Shep landed heavy blows into the old punching bag hanging in the barn.

Thud. Thud. Thud.

His ratty T-shirt was soaked with sweat.

He'd turned the general down. He was retired. He'd left the military because he'd had nothing left to give.

He just wanted to be left alone.

In his head, he saw the faces of his friends. Tortured and killed by the Taliban. Good men who'd risked everything, and never came home to their families. Shep, Vander, and the rest of their team had barely rescued their other Ghost Ops buddy Boone in time.

But Shep had been too late to rescue Julio, Miles, and Charlie.

Shep landed another punch into the bag. After they'd saved Boone, Shep had gotten reckless, he'd taken risks. More than usual.

Vander had read him the riot act after one mission had left Shep with some new bullet holes.

You're going to get yourself killed. You think Miles, Julio, and Charlie want that? You're going to get someone else killed if you don't stop the reckless behavior.

Pausing, Shep swiped his arm across his sweaty forehead.

Yeah, he'd struggled with the loss of his friends. Boone had, as well. Boone had been wrestling with some pretty heavy survivor's guilt. He'd come out of those Taliban caves alive, while the others hadn't. Recently, Boone had been on the run with a woman he was protecting. But he hadn't just protected her. No, he'd fallen in love with the woman—Gemma. Boone had found a way to move forward and live.

You need to stop hiding on this mountain, Shep.

Vander's voice again. Shep's jaw tightened. He was different than Boone. Guilty for other reasons...and the truth was, Shep had been broken long before he'd joined the military.

He knew the best way for him to move forward was to be alone. With no people to bother him. No people depending on him.

And he was not going alone into some stinking jungle to rescue the president's daughter.

The image of Hayden Sinclair's face popped into his head. That secret smile, those intelligent, brown eyes that contrasted with her golden hair.

Had they hurt her?

Fuck. He landed another flurry of blows into the bag.

The rumble of a truck engine outside caught his ear. Maybe the general had returned? Shep knew he was staying at the local motel, and hoping to change Shep's mind.

His cellphone was on the workbench, so he hadn't heard his sensors go off. Too deep in his head.

He pulled the wraps off his hands and headed to the barn door. Cool air washed over him. They'd get some snow soon.

A big, black Ford F-150 pulled to a stop.

Then he saw the man who knifed out of the truck, and his spine stiffened.

Hell.

"You're a long way from San Francisco," Shep growled.

Vander Norcross headed in Shep's direction.

He wore dark jeans and a brown leather jacket. He moved like a predator—agile, athletic, and ready for anything. Shep had never met a man like Vander before. So alert, and attuned to everything. It had made him a damned good Ghost Ops commander, and a legend.

He had dark good looks, thanks to his Italian-American heritage. And he radiated an aura of power. A man used to giving orders and having them followed.

"She needs your help."

Shep blew out a breath. "Good to see you too, Vander."

Vander gripped Shep's hand, and they shook. Intensity throbbed off him. He'd always been intense.

"It's always good to see you. Wish you'd take me up on my invitation to come to San Francisco."

"Trade this for the city?" Shep waved at the mountains and trees around him. "No, thanks."

Vander nodded. "It's not a bad spot... If you aren't hiding."

"I'm *not* hiding." His voice was harsh. They'd had this argument before.

Muttering, Shep headed toward his cabin.

It was still damaged from the fight he and Boone had fought with the team of mercenaries after Gemma. One cabin was in ruins, others peppered with bullet holes. He was slowly repairing them.

Shep slid his hands in his pockets. "How's Brynn?"

A rare smile crossed Vander's handsome face as he fell in step with Shep. "She's great. She's busy on an undercover case, at the moment."

"And you left the city?" The man was protective as hell of his wife.

Vander's smile widened. "She's undercover in a dog grooming ring that's stealing purebred puppies. One breeder got himself killed, and my wife is going to bring them all down."

Shep laughed, trying to imagine Vander's police detective wife grooming dogs. "She might bring a puppy home."

Vander snorted. "I keep her too busy for a puppy."

Shep opened the cabin door. "Coffee?"

"Sure. Colder here than in San Francisco."

"Sounds like you're going soft."

"Maybe."

There was nothing soft about the man. Vander ran Norcross Security, and kept his finger on the pulse of San Francisco. He and his team of badasses kept their friends, family, and clients safe.

"Guess I've just learned that it's okay to be soft in certain situations," Vander said.

Shep headed for the kitchen. "Easy when you have a beautiful wife."

"You should try it."

"Feel free to loan Brynn to me any day."

There was a dangerous flash in Vander's dark blue eyes. "Not with my wife, but you could find your own woman."

"The *last* thing I want is a woman. They need attention, they want things, they're demanding."

"The trick is to find a good one."

Shep grunted. "Fuck, no."

Vander pulled a slim file out from under his coat and set it on the table. "I don't need any coffee, Shep." He tapped the file. "A dossier on Hayden Sinclair."

Shep tensed. "Vander—"

"She's smart. Dedicated to her career. Barely tolerates politics. Close to her father, especially after the death of her mother." He paused. "Have you seen your mom lately?"

"No." Shep's gut twisted. He hadn't seen her in years and had no plans to change that.

Vander pushed the file toward Shep. "You're hiding up here avoiding life. I warned you I wouldn't let you keep doing that."

"Screw you, Vander. You have a beautiful wife, a successful business, a close family. You have it so easy—"

"It wasn't always easy." Vander's voice cut like a blade. "Once, I was just like you. I just did my hiding in the middle of the city and my family. Holding myself apart. Changing it doesn't happen without some effort. Without letting people who give a fuck about you help you out."

Shep stared at the wooden floor, his gut twisting.

"You have a beautiful spot here, Shep, but it's a cage. You have no purpose." Vander tapped the file again. "You are one of the few men I know can do this. The only man I know who also needs it. You can save a life, and maybe your own in the process."

HAYDEN HEARD the door scrape open.

The thud of her heart was so loud. She was still blindfolded, her wrists tied in front of her, and she was sitting on what felt like a dirty floor.

Male voices spoke in Spanish, but they talked so fast that she could barely keep up. They'd kept her locked up for the last day. She'd napped in fits and starts, but she was tired, hungry, and thirsty.

Not to mention afraid.

And filled with grief.

Maria. The pain slashed at her like sharp knives. It made it hard to breathe. She couldn't believe Maria was gone. She'd been such a good woman, a good friend.

There was a clatter as something was dropped down beside her.

The hood was pulled off. "Eat."

She blinked in the dim light. She was in a small, empty room. Simple wooden walls and a scratched-up, wooden floor. A short man with greasy black hair stood over her. He had a large nose.

A metal plate of food sat beside her, and a cup of water. The food was some simple rice dish that looked sticky and gluey.

She was so thirsty, and she awkwardly grabbed the cup with her tied hands. She drank it fast.

The man laughed at her and left. The door thumped closed behind him.

They knew who she was. Whatever they had planned wouldn't be good. She swallowed. Her father had warned her that relationships with Nicaragua were tense. He hadn't wanted her to come here.

She knew he couldn't send in a team to rescue her.

Her belly did a sickening turn.

Well, she wasn't going to just sit here and be afraid. She needed to escape.

Hayden lifted her chin. She wasn't going to just sit here and feel sorry for herself either. She ate a bit of the sloppy food, then started work on the rope tied around her wrists.

Maria and the other Secret Service agents had given her some basic self-defense training and tips over the years. She'd hoped that she'd never need it.

Maria. Hayden breathed through the pain.

For Maria, she was getting out of here. She was going to make sure the bastards behind this paid for what they'd done.

There was a small window in the room, covered by a ratty piece of cloth. There was light around the edges. She guessed they'd had her about twenty-four hours.

They'd snatched her from the dig in the morning, so it now had to be the morning of the next day.

All those researchers who'd been shot. Dr. Stephenson. Poor Lewis. It was all her fault. Her father was right, she shouldn't have come down here.

The ropes loosened a little.

Yes.

She felt a spurt of hope.

Then she heard footsteps in the hall outside and froze. Her heart pounded like a drum in her head. Thankfully, they passed by.

Her shoulders sagged. She had no idea how many abductors there were, or where she was exactly. They'd driven away from the dig site, and they couldn't have travelled more than thirty minutes. She was still in the South Caribbean Coast Autonomous Region of Nicaragua.

She dragged in a deep breath. She was all alone, but she wasn't giving up. Maria and the others deserved justice. And Hayden wanted to see her dad again.

She kept working on the ropes. Her wrists were rubbed raw, and one was bleeding a little, but it didn't stop her.

When the rope finally slipped free, she almost cried out. She bit her lip to stay silent.

Then she pushed to her feet. She quickly glanced out the window and saw a wall of jungle vegetation. The house she was in was situated in a tiny clearing surrounded by jungle. She didn't see any guards anywhere.

They were expecting her to be soft. Just the spoiled daughter of the president.

She lifted her chin. They'd regret every bad decision they'd made today.

Carefully, she crossed the room to the door and cracked it open. She heard the murmur of voices, but didn't see anyone in the narrow hallway. She slipped out, trying to be quiet.

It looked like a simple wooden house. Voices came from what she guessed was the living area.

She licked her lips, her pulse pounding. Turning, she went in the opposite direction. There were two other rooms. One was bare, and the other was filled with junk. She saw upturned beds leaning against the wall, dirty mattresses, boxes piled haphazardly. Then, at the end of the hall, she spied the back door.

Her heart leaped into her throat. She wanted out of here. She reached the door and opened it a little—

Just as a guard strolled past outside, holding a rifle.

She froze. She didn't dare move. He wasn't looking at the door, thankfully, and just kept walking.

Someone called out to him, and another guard appeared. He was smoking, and strolled up to the first one. He was also armed.

Dammit. They were right outside. She couldn't go out this way, and she couldn't go through the living room where the others were.

Think, Hayden.

She sucked in a breath. She'd make them *think* she'd left. They'd race out to find her, then she could escape for real.

Quickly, she moved back to the room with all the junk. She slid in behind a mattress that was up on its side.

It felt like sliding into a little hidey hole, but she knew her captors weren't far away. There was a chance they'd find her.

Every instinct screamed at her to run, to get away.

She dragged in a deep breath. *Patience.* Maria had always said keeping a cool head in a bad situation made the difference. Fear and adrenaline made that hard.

Hayden pulled her knees to her chest and pressed her face to her knees. She tried to relax.

She had to wait for the right moment. When her captors realized she was gone, then she'd make a run for it into the jungle.

She pulled in a shaky breath. Damn, she felt so alone. She rubbed her cheek on her knee.

You like it like that, remember? No one to lie to you or betray you.

That's right. She knew she could depend on herself.

You've got this.

CHAPTER THREE

T he helicopter swept in low over the jungle.
Shep checked his pack and rifle. He was only going in with what he could carry.

The CIA had narrowed down Ms. Sinclair's approximate location. Now he needed to do some recon, and try to get her out.

A part of him was worried he'd be dragging a hysterical woman through the jungle, but he'd read her file. Surely a woman who'd been on several archeological digs wasn't made of glass.

He huffed out a breath and pulled on his backpack. It wasn't big—he had to move fast—but it was enough to hold a few necessities.

"Almost at the drop point, *señor*," the pilot called back.

The smiling, young Nicaraguan man did some work for the CIA. He'd agreed to drop Shep in.

Shep nodded. He still wasn't sure this was a good

idea, but he wasn't letting any woman end up in the hands of the Taliban.

He saw a long, dark river snaking through the landscape. In the distance, there were some cleared areas. Probably farmland.

The helicopter slowed, and lowered. It hovered over a patch of long, thick grass.

"Thanks." He waved at the pilot, then leaped out.

He landed, then glanced upward, the downwash from the helicopter ruffling his hair. Through the cockpit window, he saw the pilot salute before pulling away.

The clearing was all waist-high grass, but surrounding it was a wall of dense jungle. The dig site was several kilometers to the east. Intel suggested that the kidnappers hadn't moved the president's daughter too far. They were waiting for the potential buyers to arrive in-country, before they moved her closer to the capital of Managua.

Shep broke into a jog, checking his direction on his compass. He'd get close to the CIA's suggested location, then scope things out.

It didn't take long for him to find his rhythm. He kept in shape, and didn't mind running. It helped clear the head.

He moved through the trees, birds squawking overhead. He adjusted course a few times. As he neared the location, he slowed, moving more stealthily. He didn't want anyone to know he was here.

He crept through the trees and spotted a dilapidated house partway down a gentle slope. There was a guard strolling around outside, with a rifle on his shoulder.

Hello, there. Shep paused, then moved to a nearby tree and gripped a branch. He climbed up higher, then settled on a thicker limb. From here, he had a decent view of the house. He pulled his binoculars out of his pack.

Sitting still, he watched and waited. There were two guards outside, neither one of whom looked like they were expecting trouble. He tried to see inside the house.

No luck. The windows were covered. *Damn.* How many more armed guards were there? And was Hayden Sinclair here, or were these just run-of-the-mill drug runners? He knew that Nicaragua was a key part of the pipeline for drugs heading from South America to the US.

Shadows moved behind one curtain at the end of the house. A third man came out to talk with the two exterior guards. The three of them joked and laughed together.

Yeah, killing and kidnapping were so funny. Sweat dripped down the side of Shep's head and he swiped at it before he pulled out his water bottle and sipped. He kept watching, and eventually, the third man went back inside the house. A mosquito buzzed around Shep's head and he slapped at it.

He remembered why he hated the jungle.

Suddenly, shouts erupted from inside the house.

Shep stiffened and grabbed his rifle.

The guards were running, then three more men burst out of the house, all with weapons in hand.

He was too far away for him to hear what they were saying, but they were agitated. One was waving his arms around.

They all scanned the area, then jogged off toward the trees in different directions.

Shep tensed. Had Hayden escaped? His frown deepened. No, he'd been watching, and he hadn't seen her.

He waited silently as one of the guards moved beneath his tree, then disappeared into the jungle.

Time to take a look inside the house.

He climbed down the tree, then headed silently toward the house. He paused at the tree line...and watched a woman slip out of the house.

His eyebrows rose. He recognized Hayden Sinclair instantly, even with the dirty face and clothes. She glanced around, then looked up at the sky. She turned left and ran for the trees.

Holy fuck. She'd just tricked her captors and escaped.

He felt a shot of grudging respect. Shaking his head, he took off after her.

She was already in the trees and trying to be quiet, but he easily followed her trail.

He circled around her, keeping an ear out for any of her abductors. He heard her mutter a curse, then he stepped out in front of her.

"I—"

Her head whipped up, and her brown eyes went wide. Without warning, she launched herself at him and slammed a respectable punch into his gut.

Shit. Shep wasn't expecting it and grunted.

"Let me go, asshole!" She tried to hit him again.

He wrapped an arm around her and lifted her off her feet. She wriggled and fought.

"Listen," he said. "Your—"

Her elbow connected with his jaw. Shep saw stars and staggered backward. Attempting to hold her flailing body, combined with the pain rocketing through his jaw, sent him off balance.

He went down and they both landed in the mud.

SHE WAS HALF TRAPPED under a very large, heavily muscled man.

Hayden fought like crazy.

She *had* to get free. She had to run.

She jabbed an elbow back, and connected with something. She heard the giant grunt again, and tried to crawl out from under his weight.

A hand gripped her leg, and dragged her back. She kicked, gritting her teeth.

"Fucking hell," her captor bit out.

Hayden kept fighting, adrenaline surging through her. She didn't stop to wonder why he was cursing in English.

"*Enough,*" he growled. He flipped her over, and his big body covered hers. She found her arms pinned above her head and pressed into the muddy ground.

She stared up into a rugged, tanned face covered by a dark beard, and a set of furious, green eyes.

"Hayden, I'm here to rescue you."

She stilled and noted two things. One, his deep voice was little more than a growl. And two, he had an American accent.

"You're American?"

"Yes. Your father sent me."

Oh, God. A mix of emotions surged through her in a vicious tangle. "Why didn't you start with that?"

His head jerked, and his eyes narrowed. "Why didn't I...?" He shook his head. "I was *trying* to, but you punched me."

"I was *abducted* and I'm fighting for my life. You should've talked faster."

"I try to talk as little as possible."

"I believe it." From the look of his scowl, he certainly had a surly thing going on.

His dark brows drew together. "You're pretty annoying for someone who needs rescuing."

"You're pretty annoying yourself, and I don't need rescuing, because I just rescued myself."

He muttered something and rose. Grudgingly, he held out a hand.

Grudgingly, she took it. He was even taller than she'd realized. She was five foot six, so she was average height. He was much bigger.

She could see now that he was clearly military. Fit body, the military gaze—alert and ready for anything. But he blended more with the short, dark beard and black hair. He also didn't have the super-straight posture like a Marine.

"Special forces," she said.

He grunted, flinging mud off his arm.

"I'd guess Delta," she added.

His gaze met hers. "Ready to get out of here, or would you like to punch me again? Maybe try a kick or two?"

She crossed her arms. "I'm ready when you are, Rambo."

"Follow me and stay close."

"All right—"

There was the sound of a twig snapping. A body flew out of the trees, a rifle aimed their way.

Her rescuer shoved her, and she stumbled into some bushes.

Then Rambo attacked.

Grunts and thuds echoed through the trees. Crouched on the ground, Hayden watched as her Delta man rammed several fast blows into the other man's head. He followed it with a headbutt.

The crack made her wince.

The Nicaraguan attacker looked stunned, his eyes blinking rapidly. He was the guy who'd brought her food. Her rescuer grabbed one of the man's arms, then twisted it. The man made a squawk, then Rambo shoved the man backward. There was the snap of bone, and her kidnapper screamed.

Her rescuer followed with another blow to the man's head, then tossed him into some bushes. The kidnapper didn't get up.

The big guy turned, his face set in hard lines. "His friends probably heard that. We should go. Fast."

He wasn't even breathing heavily. She nodded.

"Keep up." He grabbed her wrist, then headed into the trees.

Hayden jogged to keep up with his long strides. They ran through the trees and vines, moving quickly.

Somewhere nearby, she heard shouts and a whistle.

"Keep moving, Hayden."

"I am." She paused. "What's your name?"

He didn't answer.

"Fine, I can call you Rambo."

He shot her a grumpy look. "Shep."

"I'd say it's nice to meet you, Shep, but it's not, really."

"Ditto. Now move."

He pushed a hard pace, and Hayden refused to complain.

The terrain wasn't easy. The vegetation was thick, the ground uneven. They ran on and on, until it felt endless.

A wave of dizziness hit Hayden, and she swallowed. She was so thirsty and hungry, but there was no way she'd slow down.

The shouts of her abductors had faded, and she started to feel a little better.

She was getting out of here, thank God. Shep might be a huge grump of a man, but she was glad he was with her.

The man could fight.

Another wave of dizziness hit, and she gritted her teeth.

Then suddenly the ground was flying up at her, and she landed smack down on her front. The air was knocked out of her, and her vision swam.

"Hayden?" Shep crouched and pulled her up to a sitting position.

She blinked at him.

"Damn, you've got no color in your face." He held out

31

a water bottle. "Are you hurt?"

She shook her head. She took the bottle and drank greedily. When she looked up, he had a huge scowl on his face.

"When did you last drink?" he demanded.

She frowned. "They gave me a cup of water."

"In the entire twenty-four hours?" He cursed. "You're dehydrated. You should've told me."

"Running for our lives seemed more important."

"I'd prefer not to carry you. Sip slowly." He pulled a granola bar out of his backpack. "Eat."

"I see you prefer communicating in one-word sentences."

He shot her a look. Hmm, it was extremely satisfying to poke at him. It made her feel a bit better.

Kept her mind off the situation.

She nibbled the bar, and her stomach grumbled. He tore a packet open, and she looked up to see him emptying the sachet into another water bottle.

"Electrolytes. Drink it."

Hayden was feeling steadier already now. She sipped the drink. "Sorry. I should've told you I felt dizzy. I wasn't thinking clearly."

His rugged face relaxed a little and he nodded. "Can you keep moving? We need to put more distance between us and them."

She nodded.

"Good. Let's move."

CHAPTER FOUR

S hep kept an eye on his charge as they trekked through the dense jungle. The place was alive with noise, and the humidity was rising. Through a few breaks in the trees, he could see clouds were building overhead. They'd get a storm soon.

Great, just what he needed. To be stuck in the jungle in the pouring rain.

Hayden's color was better, and she hadn't complained once. She just kept walking.

Sensing his gaze, she glanced his way. "What's the plan?"

"We'll put a bit more distance between us and them, then I call for a pickup on my sat phone."

"Why not call now?"

"Could be traced."

Her eyebrows shot up. "The guys that took me didn't seem particularly sophisticated."

"It's not them I'm worried about."

She watched him, then sighed. "More info, Shep. Who are you worried about?"

"The potential buyers."

She stopped. "Buyers?"

"They put you up for sale. There are a lot of terrorist groups, and less-friendly countries, who'd like to have you as a bargaining chip. Hoping to force one of the most powerful men in the world to do what they want."

Color drained from her face.

"Hey." He gripped her arm. "I got you out. You're safe."

"I got myself out." She touched her temple, rubbing like it ached.

"You should never have been here," he said.

"I was doing my job." Her eyes sparked. "I specialize in Central American history. I can't do that without visiting Central America."

"You put lives at risk. You put your own life at risk. It's stupid."

"We took precautions. I came under an alias..." Her voice drifted off, and Shep didn't like the look on her face. "Do you know how many people were killed at the dig?"

"No."

"They killed my friend. My Secret Service agent. They shot her in front of me." Hayden's face crumpled. "Maria was a good person."

There was raw grief etched on Hayden's face. She cared. Discomfort welled in him. He didn't like seeing her so upset. "She was with you a long time?"

Hayden looked at the trees. "Over ten years."

"I'm sorry."

"You just said it was my fault." She stomped onward, flicking vegetation out of her way.

"I didn't say that." Exactly. He grabbed her shoulder. "Hayden—"

He waited until her dark eyes met his. They were filled with misery.

"Only one person is to blame for your friend's death, and that's the man who pulled the trigger." Shep cleared his throat. "I've lost friends, too. I know it sucks."

She eyed him. "In the military?"

"Yeah."

"I'm sorry you lost your friends."

He nodded. That was one topic he wouldn't be discussing with her. "Let's keep moving."

They trudged on. Shep checked his watch. Soon, he'd make the call.

"What branch of the military are you?" she asked.

"I'm not."

"What? You are definitely military, or I'll happily eat my boots."

"I left. Two years ago."

"Right." She nodded her head. "They sent you in, so if we're caught, you aren't active military and aren't on a sanctioned mission."

"Right."

"Why did you come?"

"Because they asked nicely."

She snorted. "Don't tell me that under all that gruff is a man who'd risk his life for a woman he doesn't know."

Shep grunted and didn't meet her gaze.

"So was I right when I guessed you were Delta."

He shot her a quick look.

She smiled. "I'm right. I've been around members of all branches of the military for years. I know the tells."

"I did a stint in Delta."

"A stint?" Her gaze narrowed. "Then you did something else. There isn't much else after Delta." She made a noise. "And you're the man my father chose to rescue me."

"Oh, now you're admitting I rescued you?"

"I admit nothing." She stopped. "Wait. Don't tell me you were Ghost Ops."

He met her gaze. "I can neither confirm nor deny."

Her eyes went wide. "The boogeymen of the special forces. The toughest and the best."

Shep stayed silent. Instead, he pulled out the water bottle and handed it to her.

"Okay, stay all brooding and silent." She unscrewed the top and prepared to take a sip. "Shep?"

He turned his head.

"Thanks for coming." She took a quick drink, then handed the bottle back to him. She set off again.

He watched her. Okay, more truthfully, he watched her fit, rounded ass, and nipped-in waist.

He jerked his gaze away.

She's your job. She's the president's daughter. She just survived an abduction.

Shaking his head, he shoved the water bottle away and followed her.

They trekked on in silence. Shep stayed alert for any unwanted company.

Soon, he'd call for that pickup. Just a little bit longer.

Thank God that despite her sharp tongue, Hayden Sinclair was no hothouse flower. This rescue operation was going far smoother than he'd anticipated.

She'd fooled her abductors, and it was clear she was no stranger to a hike in the jungle.

Suddenly, Shep realized something was wrong. The birds had gone silent. He grabbed the back of Hayden's shirt.

She jerked to a halt, and shot him an annoyed look over her shoulder. But as she took in his face, annoyance drained away.

Shep couldn't see or hear anything, but his instincts were shouting loudly. He yanked Hayden to him, and she made a soft gasp. Then he sank down into the dense bushes, pulling her with him.

She was flush against his chest, practically sitting in his lap. He tapped a finger to her mouth. She nodded, which rubbed her lips against his callused fingertips.

Shit. He felt the reaction, and fought hard to ignore it. Now was not the time or place to notice how soft her lips were.

Hell, it had been far too long since he'd gotten laid.

He choked the flash of desire, and forced himself to focus. There would never be a time or place where he explored her sweet mouth.

There was a rustle. He froze, and Hayden did too.

As they watched, a man crept slowly through the trees.

Hayden sucked in a breath, and Shep felt it under his palm. He kept his laser focus on the man. It was one of the guards from the house, and he moved well. He knew this territory. He might not be military trained, but he was a man of the jungle.

The man paused for a second, and Shep felt how tense Hayden was. She gripped his forearm hard.

Then the man moved on, swallowed up by the vegetation.

Finally, she sagged against Shep. He pressed his mouth to her ear. "We'll wait. To make sure he's out of range."

She nodded, and his lips brushed the delicate shell of her ear. Knots formed in his gut.

She was sitting on him—a curvy, fit package. His body didn't seem to care that her clothes and face were dirty.

Lock it down, Barlow.

He gritted his teeth together, and stared at the trees.

AS A SMALL BRANCH slapped her in the face, Hayden sighed.

Her body ached, and she was tired and hungry.

Yeah, but you're alive, and Maria and the others aren't.

Tears welled. She couldn't let it hit her. Not yet. Not until she was safe.

Shep was charging ahead of her. He didn't look a little bit tired. He just kept going—unstoppable.

"Break."

She was getting used to his use of as few words as possible.

Hayden stopped and accepted the water bottle he

held out. This time, however, he also pulled a heavy-duty satellite phone out of his backpack.

He turned away, and she heard him murmur a bunch of words that made no sense. She guessed it was a code of some kind.

Finally, he ended the call and turned back. "Our flight is inbound. We need to travel a few more klicks."

She glanced around. "We're out of range of my abductors?"

He nodded. "But I'm not taking any chances."

Shep struck her as a guy who took risks, but assessed every bit of that risk first.

She screwed the lid back on the bottle. Soon, they set off again, but this time she felt energized. It wouldn't be much longer, and she'd be out of here.

Relief was a warm burst in her chest.

"So, where do you live, Shep?"

He stayed silent.

"Let me guess. Alone in a cave. You just come out when someone sends you the bat signal."

He grunted.

The man was well-versed in grunts, shrugs, and piercing looks.

"I'm just making conversation," she said. "You know, like normal people."

He heaved out a sigh. "Colorado."

"A mountain man." She nodded. "That makes sense."

"You?"

"I'm not a mountain man."

That earned her a dry look.

"I'm at Georgetown University. I have an apartment

near the campus. It's not really home, just a place to keep my stuff." She pulled a face. "My father would prefer I live with him, which isn't happening."

"You like being on digs?"

"Yes, I love it."

But not if it cost lives. She bit her lip. "You're right. It's my fault my Secret Service agent and the others were killed." The enormity of it hit her hard.

Shep huffed out a breath and stopped so suddenly that she ran smack into the back of him. The guy was all rock-hard muscle.

"It's *not* your fault. The guys who killed them are to blame."

Was he trying to make her feel better? "You don't believe that. You said I shouldn't have been here."

"You should've had more security."

As far as she could see, that would've meant more people would have been killed.

She turned away and kept walking. For now, she couldn't let all the choking emotions of guilt and grief free. She could hear the sound of rushing water now. There had to be a river nearby.

"So, what do you do when you aren't rescuing women from the jungle?" she asked.

More silence.

She rolled her eyes. "You know, what do you do for fun?"

"Fun?" He said the word like it was a foreign concept.

"Yes, Shep. Fun." God, talking with the guy was like pulling teeth.

He scowled. "I tinker on my land. I'm restoring an old truck."

"Alone?"

"That's how I like it."

"I get that. People can be fucking exhausting sometimes."

He looked at her with a faint smile. "We can agree on that."

"Believe me, I've had my fill of fake, simpering people."

He laughed, although it sounded rusty as hell. "With your father being president, I imagine you have."

"I almost married one of them. Luckily, he showed his true colors in time."

She felt Shep watching her. God, why did she bring Dillon up?

"Marriage is for idiots," Shep said.

"Ahh, I knew you were a romantic." She glanced his way. "It happens, however, that I agree with you one hundred percent."

They reached the riverbank. The dark water was flowing swiftly, and branches and vines dangled over the water's edge. It wasn't too wide at this point.

Shep scanned the far bank. "We need to head a few klicks downstream to reach the rendezvous point."

"Who are we rendezvousing with?"

He just grunted.

She rolled her eyes. "Shep, really, you shouldn't talk so much."

Suddenly, he moved and tackled her. She landed in

the vegetation on her back, with Shep's heavy weight on top of her. A stick poked her in the shoulder.

With the hell?

He moved into a crouch, a handgun in his hand.

Her head was spinning. "What is it?" she whispered.

He pulled her against him. "Look to your right and up. In the tree branch."

She glanced up, and stiffened. "Oh, my fucking God."

It was a jaguar.

The dark feline's powerful body was sprawled on a thick branch, lazy as could be. Its tail flicked slowly, and she realized it knew exactly where they were.

Actually, the cat reminded her of Shep—big, dark, powerful, and ready to explode into action.

"Back away slowly." He kept the handgun aimed.

Hayden moved backward very, very slowly. She knew there were jaguars in Nicaragua, but also that they were quite rare.

Shep kept a tight hold on her hand, and dragged her away. They kept moving backward until the big cat was out of sight. Finally, he stopped.

Hayden's heart was pumping fast, energy singing through her veins.

"Jesus." She gripped his arm.

"That was close."

"Do you think it would've attacked us?"

"I have no idea."

She slapped a hand to his chest, a semi-hysterical laugh bubbling.

His brow creased. "You okay?"

"Hell, no."

"You're fine," he growled. "Don't lose it now."

A laugh burst out of her. "I got my friends killed, I got abducted and held hostage, I'm running for my life, and I was almost attacked by a jaguar. I'm entitled to lose it."

His scowl deepened. "I don't want to carry you. And I hate crying, so don't you fucking lose it."

"You're such an asshole." She shook her head.

Shep shrugged a shoulder. "I never said I wasn't."

She pressed the heels of her hands to her eyes and laughed again.

The grump had one thing going for him—he didn't lie. What you saw was what you got.

"Okay, I'm almost under control." She dragged in some deep breaths. "Distract me."

"How?"

"I don't know—"

A big hand cupped her face, and her words cut off.

"You're fine," he said.

She nodded. His fingers were a little rough, his green gaze piercing. His eyes were a dark shade of green with a darker rim. Hayden felt the jungle recede, and her heart kicked harder in her chest.

He was big and strong, and smelled of perspiration. That shouldn't be sexy.

"Just breathe," he said.

"That's very Zen of you." She was trying to hide her racing pulse. "Not what I expected from Mr. Ex-Military-Tough-Guy."

"You ever stop talking?"

"I talk a normal amount, but since you're at the low

end of the conversation scale, I seem chatty." She cocked her head. "I can't figure you out, Shep."

"I'm pretty self-explanatory. I'm not complicated at all. I have no secrets."

Now she made a sound. "I think you have all kinds of secrets that you never share."

His fingers stroked her cheek, and she shivered.

"You don't want my secrets, Hayden." His voice was gruff, and he stepped back, his hands dropping away. "Now come on. We can't stop."

CHAPTER FIVE

S hep wanted out of this damn jungle. He slapped at a mosquito buzzing around his head.

He wanted to deliver Hayden Sinclair safely to her father, then get the hell back to his mountain.

She kept talking to him. He'd touched her face, and her skin was so soft. He didn't always find her annoying.

The river gurgled over some rocks, and refocused his attention. He was hoping to find a place to cross it without swimming.

"Why did you leave the military? Seems like your skills are still sharp. You're good at this."

His jaw clenched, and he stayed silent.

She gave a gusty sigh. "If someone asks you a question, you're supposed to answer."

His right hand flexed. "I started to not care anymore."

Now she was silent, except for her footsteps. The woman couldn't move silently at all.

"Something bad happened?"

Acid burned in Shep's stomach. "Yeah."

"Sorry, Shep. I was just making conversation. I didn't mean to tread somewhere dark."

He paused, examining the pressure building in his chest. Hell, he sort-of felt like sharing.

Then she let out a sharp gasp.

He whirled, whipping his rifle up.

But there were no intruders.

"Look." She pointed.

There was a dugout canoe on the river, tied to a branch. It was empty, just bobbing on the water.

He scanned the nearby jungle and didn't see anyone.

He hurried over and quickly untied it. "Get in."

"We can't just steal it. Some poor local—"

"Get in, Hayden."

"Fine, fine." She stepped one foot in, caught her balance, then shifted to the front of the canoe. Shep leaped in and let the current take it.

He grabbed the rough-hewn paddle, and sat down. He sliced the paddle through the water.

"How far do we need to go?" she asked.

"Not far. This will speed things up."

Hayden curled up into herself, staring at the wall of green. She looked lost in her head.

Shep looked away. She'd be out of here soon and no longer his responsibility. Then he spotted the glistening track sliding down her cheek.

Hell. Tears made him feel useless. He pressed his lips together. It wasn't his business if she wanted to cry.

Against his will, his gaze moved back to her. He sighed. "Hayden?"

She looked up, and swiped at her eyes. "Sorry."

"Nothing to be sorry about."

"God, you're being nice to me. You must think I'm going to lose it again."

"No, I don't." He suspected that under Hayden Sinclair's soft skin lay pure steel. She was far tougher than he'd expected.

She sighed. "I was thinking of Maria. She was such a good person. A nagger extraordinaire." Hayden gave a watery laugh. "She's just gone. Ended. Erased. And for what?" She hit the side of the boat. "It's *so* unfair. And I'm angry, sad, and devastated."

He saw the misery on her face. He stopped paddling, and reached over and gripped her knee. "I told you I get it. I lost friends. Good friends. We were like brothers, and they were some of the best men I ever knew."

She bit her lip. "In Afghanistan?"

He gave her a nod, chest tight. Talking about the guys always hurt. "Our team was ambushed. Four of them were taken hostage." And had unspeakable things done to them. "We tried to find them. It took us twenty hours." Twenty long, fucking hours. He dragged in a breath. Every hour had felt like an eternity. "By the time we found them, there was only one left alive."

"I'm so sorry, Shep." She put her hand over his. "It's the worst to be helpless. I went through something similar when my mom died of cancer. There's nothing you can do to bring them back, and all we can do is feel how much we miss them. And second-guess everything, and drown in the guilt."

He met her gaze. He'd never, ever met a woman who knew exactly how he felt. He cleared his throat. "I'm

47

guessing your Maria loved her job. Protecting someone she cared about. She knew the risks, Hayden. My guys did, too. I try to remember that."

She gave him a faint smile. "That's the most you've ever said in one go, I think."

"I see your smartass tendencies are still okay."

Then a sound caught his ear. He cocked his head.

She shifted, following his example.

Shep frowned. Then he realized what it was. *Oh, fuck.*

With the paddle, he rowed them quickly to the edge of the river. Dense vegetation dangled into the water.

"Shep?" Her voice was tense.

"There's a boat coming."

She gasped. "I can hear the engine."

"Get in the water."

"What?"

"We need to hide in the water. The slope of the bank here is too steep for us to get out. It'll take us time to get up and we'll leave a trail. Get out, and I'll let the canoe drift downstream."

She pulled a face, but gripped the edge and slipped over the side. Shep followed. The water was cool.

He gave the canoe a hard shove and it drifted off.

"Underneath those bushes." He nodded his head.

She shoved through the water. "I'd better not get eaten by piranhas."

"You know the piranha thing is a myth." He sloshed past her.

"Yes, but it's hard to ignore it when you're neck-deep in a Central American river."

The drone of the boat engine grew louder. He tugged her under the branches and let them fall back into place. He pulled her close and they sank low in the water, until only their noses, eyes, and tops of their heads were visible above the water line,

There were shouts, and the sound of the engine changed. A sleek speedboat came into view. It was filled with armed men. One man pointed down the river.

Damn. They'd spotted the canoe.

The men all spoke rapidly amongst themselves, peering in all directions.

Nothing to see here. Carry on.

One man lifted a rifle, and fired at the side of the river, into the jungle.

Hayden jolted, and Shep tightened his hold on her. She pressed her face against his neck.

The idiot sprayed more bullets into the bank. Shep tensed. He was getting damn close to their hiding place. Through the plants, he saw the rifle swivel in their direction.

"*Down.*" Shep tugged Hayden under the murky water.

He moved, shielding her with his body. One stray bullet, and he knew she could end up hurt or dead.

Then the gunfire stopped. They both popped their heads up, pulling in air.

The men in the boat were clearly arguing, and gesturing frantically. They were speaking rapid Spanish, but he made out some words.

Find the woman.

Shit. His jaw tensed. They were *not* getting her.

After more arguing, one man got out of the boat. He held his rifle above his head as he sloshed towards the river's edge, not far from Shep and Hayden's hiding place.

Damn, Shep couldn't shoot him, or it would alert the others.

The man crouched by the river's edge, looking for track marks, no doubt. The boat roared off, and soon the engine sounds faded.

Shep met Hayden's gaze. He held his fingers to his lips, then pointed to the man.

She nodded, her eyes wide, and her face pale.

The man moved closer.

Shep let go of the rifle and pulled in a long, slow breath. Then he attacked, exploding out of the bushes.

The man jerked, and Shep launched himself out of the water. The man had barely turned in their direction, before Shep was on him.

Shep punched him—once, twice. The man dropped his gun with a splash.

Spinning around, Shep got an arm around the man's neck, and yanked him back into a chokehold.

The guy was smaller than Shep, but strong. Plus, he was fighting for his life.

The man jerked and struggled. They staggered along the river edge, both of them slipping in the mud.

Shep cursed. He could do without the added weight of his damn backpack. They both fell and hit the ground, sliding down the slick slope, and landed in the water with a splash.

The man thrashed, but Shep gritted his teeth and held on. Water splashed around them.

He felt his grip slipping. *Dammit*.

Suddenly, Hayden waded through the water and threw herself on the man's legs, holding him still.

Shep knew they couldn't leave the guy alive. He'd give away their location to his friends. Shep met Hayden's gaze briefly, then steeled himself. He shoved the man's head under the water.

He held him there, as the man kept thrashing. Eventually, his movements slowed; he bucked one more time, then went lax.

"Thanks." Shep rose, and dragged the man's body to the river's edge. He dumped the body in some dense vegetation.

He turned back to Hayden. "You okay?"

She was soaked, her hair sticking to her head. She pushed some strands off her face and swallowed. "I'm not entirely sure. I've never helped kill someone before."

"He would've killed me, and dragged you back to his boss."

She pressed a shaky palm to her cheek. "I know. But it's not quite so easy to just shrug it off."

"Good. You never want to get to a place where taking a life is easy."

She watched him for a long moment, her gaze piercing, then she nodded.

"All right. We need to keep moving." He splashed some water on his clothes to wash the mud off, and checked his backpack. Thankfully, it was waterproof. He stared at the river. His rifle was gone, dammit, now resting on the river bottom somewhere. He opened his pack, pulled out his handgun, then slipped it into his waistband. He took Hayden's arm. "Let's go."

Together, they scrambled up the slope, skidding a few times.

At the top, they set off through the trees.

"It's not far to the rendezvous point," he told her.

"Thank God."

They trudged on. Shep wanted to move faster, but he could tell Hayden was reaching her limit. She needed rest, sleep, and food.

"Well, at least we had an impromptu bath, I guess." She plucked at her damp shirt. "Although with this humidity, we might not dry out."

The trees thinned out. Ahead was a large, grassy clearing with waist-high grass.

"Come on, Hayden. Not far now. Once we're on the helo, you'll be getting out of here."

She made a sound. "Yes, please. I won't lie, I'm dreaming of a shower, followed by a steak and a beer."

Shep grunted. He figured the president's daughter would go for something fancier, with a glass of expensive wine.

"How do you like your steak done?" he asked.

"Medium. And preferably with a giant baked potato."

That did sound good.

As they reached the halfway point across the clearing, pushing their way through the thick grass, he scanned their surroundings for any company—both the animal and the bad-guy variety. Everything was still and clear.

A second later, a steady *thump, thump, thump* filled the air.

He froze. *Fuck.* He looked up.

"Shep?"

"There's a helicopter coming closer." It could be their pickup, but by Shep's best guess, their guy would be flying in from the opposite direction. *Shit.* "Get down!"

He grabbed her arm and yanked her to the ground. He wrapped his body around hers, and hoped the long grass would hide them. Mud squished underneath them.

Hayden was tense, tilting her head to look up at the sky.

A helicopter thundered overhead.

It was an old Huey, painted dark green. *Shit.* Not his contact.

The helo circled around, hovering above the clearing. Hayden's fingers clenched on his arm, digging in. He saw the fast rise and fall of her chest.

She was scared.

Without thinking, he slid his hand over hers. Her fingers clenched on his. She turned her head to face him.

Their faces were only an inch apart. Up close, he could see gold flecks in her brown eyes. She pressed against him. The noise of the helo made it feel like they were trapped in their own world. He let his gaze run over her face, taking it all in—high cheekbones, long lashes, that stubborn jawline.

Then she shifted and pressed her mouth to his.

Fuck.

53

Shep stiffened for a second, then he lost his mind. He cupped the back of her head and kissed her back.

Her mouth opened for him instantly. He slid his tongue inside, and hers stroked his, bold and needy. Desire shot through him and he deepened the kiss. Damn, she tasted good. Her hands slid into his hair, clenching tightly. He pressed closer and kept kissing her.

When they broke the kiss, their lips were still touching.

What the fuck?

Trying to get his head back in the game, he registered that the helicopter had moved on. He could still hear the rotors. It was nearby, moving in a search pattern.

Whoever took Hayden knew they couldn't have gone too far on foot.

He cleared his throat. "They've moved on."

She nodded.

His gaze narrowed. "You okay?"

"Mostly."

"Now's not the time to lose it."

She tried to laugh. "God, it's really bad when you being an asshole actually makes me feel better."

"I've got more asshole-ness that I can share."

She rolled her eyes.

"We should keep moving," he told her.

She rose and nodded. "I'm okay."

He watched her set her shoulders back. She just dealt with whatever got thrown at her and charged on. She kept saying she was gonna lose it, but he suspected Hayden Sinclair was tougher than anyone knew.

"Good, because I'm not your nanny."

That got him another eye roll and she slapped his chest. "Thanks, Shep. Your tender care makes me feel so much better."

But he couldn't let himself forget that he wasn't here to make her feel better, and he sure as hell wasn't here to kiss her. Not again. He was here to keep her safe.

CHAPTER SIX

Hayden followed Shep's broad back, her mind churning.

Not from the helicopter searching for them, which she thankfully couldn't hear anymore.

No, it was from that kiss.

The sizzling, crazy-hot kiss she couldn't stop thinking about.

Although Shep seemed to have put it out of his mind. She scowled at his back. He was pretending it never happened.

She'd had lots of kisses. Some good ones, some not good ones. But she'd never had one that rough and hot. One that made her forget where she was.

Forget who she was.

She felt a skitter of alarm run down her spine. After Dillon, she'd had *zero* interest in men. She didn't want a boyfriend. She didn't want anyone close enough to hurt her. And the fiasco with her ex made her realize that she didn't want to get married.

She sure as hell didn't want or need a grumpy former soldier who communicated mostly in grunts.

She touched her lips. They were still tingling.

Dammit.

She glared at his back. How dare he just ignore that kiss, though? Like he hadn't felt anything.

Her gaze wandered over his body. The man really broad shoulders. Her gaze dipped lower, below his backpack. Not to mention a very muscular ass that filled out his cargo pants just right.

Jeez, Hayden. You're in danger, and lost in the Nicaraguan jungle. Maybe focus a little?

She stared at the trees. They'd moved back into dense foliage again.

She wasn't doing any more digs outside the USA. An image of Maria's body dropping to the ground sent a fresh spike of pain through her. She still couldn't believe her friend was gone.

"Stop." Shep held up a hand.

Hayden paused and leaned on a tree trunk. She was so tired.

"We're close," he said.

Thank God.

"We'll wait here until our ride comes in."

She gave him a nod. Overhead, the birds were going crazy in the trees.

"Are we just going to ignore that kiss?" Shit, how had she let that slip out?

Shep didn't look at her, but she saw a muscle tick under his eye. "Yes."

She straightened. "Fine."

57

"Good."

"It wasn't worth mentioning anyway."

His head swiveled, his brows drew together. "Really?"

She sniffed. "Yes."

He leaned closer. "Because you were clinging pretty hard while you kissed my brains out."

Hayden gasped and took a step toward the big, annoying grump. "*You* kissed *my* brains out."

"That's not how I remember it."

"It's the truth, you big—"

His mouth crashed down on hers. Hayden heard a low, needy moan, and realized with a jolt that the sound was coming from her.

His arms closed around her, hauling her close. She slid her arms around his neck, plastering herself against him.

The kiss turned into a sizzling-hot melding of mouths.

His mouth moved over hers, urging her lips wider. She dug her fingers into his shoulders for leverage as she kissed him back. His tongue swept over hers with deep strokes, owning her mouth. His beard added to the sensations, and she liked it. A lot.

What would it feel like scraping over other parts of her body?

Somehow, her hands were in his dark hair, and he had one hand tangled in hers. Holding each other as close as possible. His mouth was firm, demanding, and she kissed him back the same way.

She felt like something wild had taken her over.

It was the distant sound of a helicopter that broke the moment.

They both pulled back, their chests heaving. The world around Hayden was a blur. For a blinding second, all she could see was Shep's face, stamped with need, his eyes blazing. She was gratified to see that he was breathing heavily, too.

He gave her a hot, annoyed look, then turned to scan the sky.

"Is it our ride this time?" Crap, her voice was low and husky.

He frowned, his gaze above the tree line. Then he nodded. "Yes."

"Thank God."

"We'll wait for him to hover out in the clearing, then we'll run out. The quicker we're out of here, the better."

"I couldn't agree more."

Turbulent green eyes met hers. "Good." Then he turned his back on her.

Ugh, he was the most annoying man she'd ever met. He sure knew how to kiss, though.

She blew out a breath. She *wasn't* thinking about that now.

Or ever.

A white helicopter hovered off the ground, bending the long grass. It rippled like water.

Shep wrapped strong fingers around her bicep. He was highly alert, continuously scanning the trees.

"Let's move."

Bent over, they jogged toward the aircraft. Relief

welled inside Hayden. She was getting out of here, and going home.

A sharp, high-pitched *whoosh* came from overhead.

She looked up, just as something hit the helicopter.

Boom.

The explosion lifted her and Shep off their feet.

Everything spun, and her ears rang painfully.

She smacked into the ground, the air knocked out of her. Shep landed beside her with a grunt.

Ow. Pain radiated everywhere and her head felt fuzzy. She blinked and tried to roll.

Then Shep was there, yanking her up.

"Run!"

FUCKING FUCK.

Keeping a grip on Hayden, Shep sprinted for the trees.

She stumbled, unable to keep up. He swung around and lifted her. He slung her across his shoulders and set off at a jog.

When he hit the tree line, he heard a second helicopter closing in.

These guys really wanted Hayden.

Well, they weren't having her.

On autopilot, he kept running. His only objective was to get Hayden as far away as possible.

She hung still and silent over his shoulders.

Shit, was she okay? He had no choice but to keep

running, until the only sounds he heard were those of the jungle.

Finally, he slowed to a walk then stopped. He swung her down and set her on her feet.

She wavered. He caught her, gaze on her face. It was pale and covered in a sheen of perspiration.

"That poor pilot," she whispered.

She needed rest. They were probably far enough away to stop for a little bit.

He scanned a large tree nearby. It had a wide base and speared high into the sky. He shoved aside some bushes growing around it and checked for any unwelcome critters.

"Sit."

This time there was no snappy comeback. She dropped down heavily to the ground.

"There's no way out," she said woodenly. "They'll keep coming. They'll keep killing."

"Hayden." He dropped to a crouch in front of her. "I'm your way out. There's no way in hell I'm letting them get their hands on you."

She drew in a shaky breath. He pulled his backpack off. Thank fuck it was waterproof or all his gear would have been drenched from the river. He handed her a water bottle.

"So many people have died already. Maria. The researchers at the dig, that pilot—" her voice cracked. "Sorry Shep, but..." Tears rolled down her face.

Damn. He had no experience with tears. He avoided relationships. He limited them to a quick, anonymous fuck. Usually, he went into Denver and hooked up with someone he met at a bar. But that wasn't very often, since he hated going to the city.

So, his experience comforting a crying woman was limited.

Once, he'd dried his sister's tears. But she'd been young and easy to cheer up.

Until she'd been murdered.

Until he'd been too late to save her from a monster.

"I'm sorry, Shep," Hayden repeated again. Her face crumpled, and she started to cry in earnest.

Hell. Her tears made him feel useless. It was the one feeling he hated most in the world.

"Come here," he said gruffly, as he pulled her onto his lap.

She instantly snuggled against him, pressing her face to his chest. She let loose small, muffled sobs.

"I don't cry, usually." She sniffed. "I'm a politician's daughter. You can't show too much emotion, or you'll be labeled unstable and hysterical. And you can't show too little, you'll be called unfeeling."

He grunted. Sounded like bullshit to him.

"I know. It's all so fake and horrible." More tears. "I can't seem to hold these ones back."

She'd been through hell over the last two days. She'd earned a few tears.

He stroked a hand down her back. Hell, he wanted her to feel better, but he had no idea how to go about that. "Just hold on. You're doing fine."

She rubbed her cheek against his shirt, and gave a hiccupping laugh. "You're being nice to me?"

"No. I'm not nice."

Her tears slowed, her gaze on his face. "I'm starting to think you are. Just a little. You just hide it."

"No." His voice was a growl.

She smiled now, and fuck, she looked beautiful, even with tears staining her cheeks.

"I think you're lying."

"I'm not, princess. I'm an asshole. Ask anyone."

She raised a brow. "Princess?"

"Yep. You're pretty much America's equivalent to a princess."

"That's the best you can do?" She shook her head.

His surliness just seemed to roll off her. He'd never met anyone like her. "You done with the crying?"

She sniffed and wiped her sleeve across her face. "I think so."

"Good. We need a new plan."

She nodded.

Sitting her down, he rifled around in his backpack and pulled out a map of the area. He pulled it out of a protective, plastic sleeve. "I think our best bet is to head southeast toward Bluefields."

"It's the largest town in the area. I've only been there once, but lots of people from the dig go there on their days off."

"It has an airfield, and it's on the coast. That gives us options. En route, I'll call a friend. See if we can line up some help and an extraction."

"Okay."

There was a rumble of thunder overhead.

Through the canopy of trees, he saw the dark clouds building. *Great, just what they needed.*

He opened his backpack and pulled out a thin raincoat. "Put this on."

"What about you?"

"I'll be fine."

She pulled on the plastic coat, as Shep checked his GPS.

"All right. It's about thirty kilometers to Bluefields."

She nibbled on her bottom lip. "That's almost twenty miles."

He nodded. "Through mostly jungle terrain. When we come across any farms, we'll need to avoid detection."

She swallowed and looked up. "There's a storm coming, and we only have a few hours until night hits."

"We won't make it tonight. We'll have to make camp. But I want to put some distance between us and your abductors."

She rubbed her temple. "Okay."

"You up for that?"

She lifted her chin. "Yes."

It wouldn't be easy, but Hayden Sinclair just kept surprising him.

CHAPTER SEVEN

H ayden was miserable.

The rain had started, and she was saturated, even with the raincoat Shep had given her. Water dripped off everything and it was steady and relentless. Her abraded wrists hurt as well, the grazes throbbing.

Emotions churned inside her, and were much worse than her physical discomfort.

They trekked through the muddy terrain, and she just focused on following Shep. He was even wetter than she was, but he didn't complain.

He didn't slow down or pause, just kept going. He'd promised to get her out, and she believed him.

It was getting dark. Soon, she wouldn't be able to see where she was putting her feet. Her brain kept running images like a movie on repeat—Maria getting shot, gunfire at the dig, being tied up in that house, Shep killing the man at the river, the helicopter exploding.

She bit her lip.

She'd had her cry. Shep had even comforted her, which she guessed wasn't something he did a lot.

Hayden stared at his immensely broad back. He'd shared about losing his friends, and she knew his time in the military had left its scars.

He stopped, and she narrowly avoided running into him.

"How are you holding up?" As his gaze ran over her, he frowned.

She must look as bad as she felt. She straightened her shoulders. "I'm fine."

That got her a grunt. He fished around in his backpack. "Here." He shoved a granola bar at her.

Her stomach revolted. "I'm not hungry."

"Eat it."

"I said—"

He huffed out a breath. "You need to keep up your strength. I'm not carrying you all the way to Bluefields."

Asshole. "*Fine.*" There was no way she wanted to slow them down, and fainting would be bad. "Would it kill you to speak in entire sentences?"

"You always a smartass?"

"Only when provoked, which isn't often. You seem to have that special skill." She leaned against a tree trunk.

"You're doing all right. I want to cover a bit more ground before we make camp."

She frowned. "Camp with what?" She really didn't relish the idea of sleeping in the rain.

He patted his backpack. "I have a tent. It'll be a tight fit, but it'll keep us dry."

"I'm starting to think that beaten-up backpack of yours is magical. Bigger on the inside than the outside."

That got her a small smile.

Her eyes widened. "Oh my God, did you just smile?"

"Nope."

"You did."

Now he scowled and she cheerfully bit into the granola bar. Unsurprisingly, it tasted like dust.

"That'll give you a bit of energy so we can go a bit farther."

She gave him a tired nod and straightened. "Onward."

They headed off again. Thankfully, the rain eased up a little, but before long, it was so dark she could barely see where she was putting her feet.

"This will do." Shep stopped in some dense trees, and opened his backpack.

"You need help with the tent?"

"I've got it."

Thank God. She was too tired to do anything.

He pulled the tiniest little package out of his backpack, and her eyebrows rose. How the hell would that fit them both?

She was surprised when the tiny package opened into a decent-sized tent. It wasn't big, but it was larger than she'd guessed. It had a simple triangular roof, and Shep put it up with practiced ease. It was a dark green that blended in with the surroundings.

He nodded his head. "Take your boots off. Once we're in, we need to get out of our wet clothes."

Hayden stilled. Get their clothes off? And be naked together in that tiny space?

"I have a clean T-shirt you can wear," he said gruffly. "We can't stay in the wet clothes, and it's important to keep your feet dry."

"I know." She climbed in and shucked her muddy boots. She set them just inside the entrance to the tent.

Once Shep climbed in, any ideas of the tent being spacious evaporated. The man was big. He dealt with his boots, then flicked her a glance. He pulled out a small towel and a clean white T-shirt.

"Dry off." Then he turned his head and stared at the tent zipper.

Right. Maneuvering to remove her wet clothes in a tight space with a giant hunk of man right beside her proved to be a frustrating challenge. Biting her tongue, she twisted her arms and lifted her hips. She was pretty sure she almost dislocated her shoulder.

"You done?" He sounded like he was gritting his teeth.

"Almost. There isn't exactly a lot of room in here." She bumped into him and felt the heat pumping off his body. "Sorry to interrupt your evening plans."

She heard him mutter under his breath and was pretty sure he said *smartass*.

Finally, she had the clean, dry shirt on. Since it was Shep's it was enormous on her. She was excruciatingly conscious that she was naked under it.

Then Shep moved, unbuttoning his shirt. Hayden snapped her eyes toward the tent wall. She listened to every sound and movement. She closed her eyes for a second, imagining what he would look like.

Then, because she was weak and couldn't stop herself, she turned her head.

The expanse of his broad back was covered in slabs of muscle and tanned skin. Her heart gave a huge thump, and her hand itched to trace the lines of muscle along his spine. Then she noticed the scars.

He had several puckered scars—some round, some long lines. *God*. So many.

He shrugged a dry shirt on, and she quickly looked away.

"Give me your wet clothes."

She turned her head. He was wearing a dry shirt and boxer shorts. *Don't look at his huge, muscular thighs*. She cleared her throat and handed him her wet clothes. She tried not to be fazed that her underwear were in the wet pile.

She watched with interest as he pulled a towel out of his magic backpack, then wrapped up their wet clothes.

"It won't dry them completely, but it'll absorb a lot of the moisture," he told her.

"Great." She smoothed her damp hair back. "Now, if you tell me that your magic bag has a steak and beer in there, I'll sell you my soul."

He made a sound that might have almost been a laugh. "No steak, but—" he fished around and pulled out a small brown packet "—I can do an MRE of beef stew."

Hayden wrinkled her nose. "I've had a few ready to eat meals. I can't say they're much fun."

"The stew's not bad."

She took it from him. He opened another one for himself.

"What's yours?"

"Chicken, vegetables, and rice. No beer, though. Sorry."

They settled down to eat, the faint pitter patter of rain dripping on the tent. Shep hadn't lied, the stew wasn't too bad. Suddenly, she was really hungry.

"So why archeology?"

She glanced up at him. "I always loved history. And if I'm truthful, when I was ten, I really wanted to be Indiana Jones." She laughed. "Then I worked out archeology isn't really like the movies, but I was still hooked on learning about the past. Uncovering small fragments of ancient civilizations is so fascinating. You become like a detective, putting the clues together. I love puzzles." She shrugged. "And those fragments, they're real. They're the truth. They aren't a picture painted by someone for propaganda, or telling a story for click bait, or a perfect image posted for likes and follows. Every time I find an interesting artifact, I decide what it tells me about a place or culture, not someone selling me their story."

Shep held her gaze. "I hate liars and posers too."

She laughed. "Sorry. Growing up in my life, I was exposed to way too many of them. It left a mark."

"Can't be easy when your father is the President of the United States."

"Now there is an understatement." Her throat tightened and the gut-wrenching reality of the last two days hit her in full force. She pressed a hand to her eyes. So many times she'd wished her father wasn't in politics, or at least not in the public eye. He wasn't to blame for this, but still, she wished things were different. She sighed. Her father believed in helping people, and she knew he was a good president.

She just wished it hadn't painted a target on her back.

"Hayden?"

She met Shep's gaze. "I hate my father's job, even though it's one he's dedicated to, and should absolutely do. I hate that it results in this. People dead, and me wet and covered in mud, and on the run. I'm pretty sure this is the last place you'd like to be, too."

He made a sound. "No one wants to be here."

She smiled briefly. "True. Where would you be if you weren't here?"

"My place. My cabin in the Rocky Mountains."

She looked at him and grinned.

His scowl deepened. "What?"

"My grumpy rescuer, you couldn't be more stereotypical if you tried. Reclusive mountain man."

"I like the mountains."

"Of course, you do. Because you can avoid people."

"Yeah."

"You can grump around and scowl at the trees."

He shook his head.

"Scare a few elk and cougars."

"Enjoying yourself?" he asked dryly.

"Funnily enough, I am." She also realized that this man made her feel safe and comfortable.

She knew that Shep didn't lie, and had a sort of bone-deep loyalty that was rare. He told you to your face exactly what he thought, even when he knew you wouldn't like it. There was no pretending, just the unvarnished truth.

"So, you have any friends that visit this cabin of yours?" she asked.

"Actually, it's cabins. The place was once an old mine site, then someone turned it into rental cabins. It went bust and I bought it for a deal when I was still in the military. Sometimes former military buddies visit."

"All Ghost Ops as well?"

"That's classified." He shot her a look. "My buddy Boone stayed recently with his now-girlfriend. Gemma was on the run from some bad guys. We had a small firefight."

He sounded excited about that.

"So, your buddy Boone has a girlfriend, what about you?" Her belly fluttered as she waited for his answer.

"You think I'd kiss you if I had a woman?"

"No, but things were kind of intense when we kissed."

"I don't have a woman. I don't want a woman. I'll never have a woman."

She cocked her head. "Why?"

"They take time and energy." He shook his head. "I'm not interested."

As he looked away, she saw something on his face. There was something more to this. Had he lost a woman —someone he loved—before?

"I don't want a man, either."

Shep's eyebrows rose.

"It's true. Relationships take time and energy, and men are usually lying, cheating bastards."

"Don't hold back."

"That ex-fiancé I had. Thankfully, I discovered he was a cheating asshole before I married him."

"He *cheated* on you?"

The simple words, said with scorn, were a balm. "Yes. He was an idiot, and I was an idiot for believing him. He had a girlfriend on the side, and he was just interested in being in my father's sphere of influence. Dillon is a lawyer with a lot of political ambition. And I fell for his crap." She shook her head. "Never again."

"Here's to freedom."

"I like that. No ball and chain for us."

"Amen to that." Shep crushed up his empty meal packet. "You should get some sleep. You've had a hellish few days and need the rest."

Hayden nodded. And despite being stuck in a tiny tent with a near-stranger, she knew with Shep beside her, she would actually sleep.

SHEP WOKE up to find himself wrapped around a warm, curvy body with his face pressed against blonde hair. He froze, and realized his hard cock was pressed against Hayden's round ass and one of his hands cupped her breast.

Shit. He couldn't quite get his brain working, fighting to let go of the last vestiges of sleep. She felt so good.

He'd never liked sharing a bed with a woman. He hated having someone else in his space. But this was... nice. She was warm and soft.

She moved, squirming against him, pressing her ass more firmly against his throbbing cock.

He barely swallowed a groan, his cock lengthening. Thank God she was asleep. If she woke up right now, she'd scream her head off.

He started to move his hand, already mourning the loss of the soft globe in his palm. Suddenly her hand shot out, gripping his wrist, and holding him still.

"I'm awake," she murmured.

Crap. "Sorry—"

"I'm not." She rubbed her ass against him again in a slow, deliberate move. "Right now, I'm warm and safe. I..." Her voice cracked. "I need that, Shep." She pressed his hand more firmly against her breast.

He closed his eyes. He didn't move, just lay there breathing in her scent. He knew this was wrong, but he couldn't make himself let her go or move away.

Tentatively, his fingers gently caressed her breast, and she made a small sound. He felt her nipple pebble against his palm.

"When we leave this tent—" she said huskily "—reality, which is horrible right now, will roll back in."

She tilted her head back, and his gaze dropped to the curve of her lips.

"I want to hold it back, just a little longer." She licked her lips. "If you're okay with that."

Shep felt a bunch of conflicting emotions. She was the president's daughter. She was in danger and depending on him. He had no right to touch her.

"It's not right." His voice sounded like gravel.

"It feels right. Besides, you strike me as a guy who does his own thing."

Fuck.

Her teeth sank into her bottom lip, her face shuttering. "If you don't want me—"

Not want her? He growled, then he shifted his head and pressed his mouth to hers. She instantly opened her lips, and he slid his tongue inside the silken warmth, kissing her deeply. He caressed her breast, rubbing her nipple between his fingers.

She moaned, undulating against him. Shep slid his palm down her body, over her belly.

"Yes." She arched into him.

Her shirt was bunched up to her waist. He didn't stop to think about how much he liked the fact that the only thing she wore was his shirt.

He slid his hands lower and found a tiny strip of hair between her thighs.

She made a hungry sound, and he rubbed his fingers against her slick folds.

"Like that?" he asked.

"Yes. God, *yes.*"

He explored her sweet pussy, before he moved his thumb up and found her clit. He rubbed it.

"Don't stop." She gripped his wrists. "Please don't stop."

He couldn't stop now if he wanted to. He worked her, drawing some of her slick juices up so he could keep working her clit, harder and harder. It swelled for him, and the way her body moved, he knew she was getting close.

The musky smell of her arousal filled the tent. Fuck, he wondered what she tasted like.

On the next circle of his fingers, she came.

He kept his gaze locked on her face, watching the pleasure cross her features, her body shaking.

When she sagged back against him, desire raged through his body.

Suddenly, she rolled over, her face flushed. She pushed him flat on his back, pressed her hands to his chest, and kissed him.

Shep couldn't think, all he could do was feel. Desire rocketed through him with each beat of his heart.

Her mouth traveled down his neck, her teeth biting into his skin.

"*Fuck*," he muttered.

Then she shifted, her hands pushing his boxer shorts down. His cock sprang free.

"Oh." Her eyes widened, and she stroked him. "Should have known a guy as big as you would have a monster cock."

Damn, it felt good. Her slim fingers pumped his hot cock. He lifted his hips, pushing into her hand.

The way she watched him, her cheeks flushed, her mouth open, made his gut even tighter. He clamped his hand over hers, and big, brown eyes met his. Together they stroked him, and he showed her just how he liked it. Fast, a little rough.

He felt the muscles in his gut tightening like wires pulled tight. He wouldn't last much longer.

They kept stroking his cock, then she slid her other hand down between his thighs and cupped his balls.

With a fierce groan, Shep came. He felt his come splatter on his stomach, and he groaned through his release.

Finally, when he was done, he flopped back, chest working like bellows. He met her gaze, expecting to see awkwardness.

Instead, she smiled at him. "Thank you."

That wasn't what he expected. Then again, Hayden Sinclair was nothing like he expected.

He reached over and grabbed his backpack. He fished around inside and pulled out a pack of wet wipes.

"I'm starting to really like your magic backpack," she said.

She took some wipes, and carefully wiped the release off his abs.

He cleared his throat. "Hayden—"

"It doesn't need to be awkward. We're two consenting adults finding pleasure. That's it." Her tone was casual and matter of fact.

She took some more wipes and turned away to clean her own body.

Something about the casual words annoyed Shep. Usually, it was his line to say something like that. For some reason he couldn't pinpoint, he didn't like Hayden saying it. Not when he was still riding the pleasure of watching her come, and her making him come.

With a shake of his head his sat up. "Get dressed. Our clothes won't be fully dry, but they'll be less wet than yesterday. We need to get moving so we can make it to Bluefields."

CHAPTER EIGHT

They'd been trekking through the jungle for over an hour, and Shep had been silent the whole time.

Hayden ducked under a branch. Her clothes were damp, but he'd given her fresh socks. As she had about a hundred times since they'd left their small camp, she studied Shep.

He'd appeared to have put the hot, sexy moment they'd shared aside.

She pulled a face. She wished she could forget.

Every second she kept reliving those rough fingers on her, stroking between her legs. She shivered.

Then she blew out a breath. She needed to focus.

Setting her shoulders back, she picked up speed. One of her wrists was throbbing, and she reached down to rub it. It was really sore. She pushed her sleeve up and saw that her skin was red. It wouldn't be too much longer and they'd be in Bluefields, and safe. It could wait.

As they walked, the humidity grew, and soon sweat was trickling down and soaking into her bra. She swiped a sleeve across her forehead, and told herself to keep walking.

Suddenly, Shep stopped and held up a hand.

She froze. Had her abductors found them?

He crept forward quietly, and she followed. Just beyond the trees was some cleared land. She could hear someone humming.

A second later, she saw a local worker not far down the cleared slope. In the distance, she spotted two small houses. It was a farm of some sort.

Shep carefully stepped back, and grabbed her arm. He pulled her away and they circled around, putting some distance between them and the farmer.

Hayden still felt tense, but slowly she relaxed.

"I want to avoid anyone seeing us," Shep said.

She nodded.

They stopped for a drink and a granola bar. God, this trek felt endless. At least it wasn't raining.

She watched as Shep ate his granola bar in two bites. He looked tired. She watched him drink, her gaze moving to his strong throat as he drank the water. Then he closed his eyes for a second.

Suspicion grew inside her. "Did you sleep last night?"

He lowered the water bottle. "I rested."

"That wasn't my question."

"I'm here to protect you. I had to stay awake to make sure no one crept up on us."

He hadn't slept. The entire night. Annoyance burned through her. "I can see that you're tired."

"I'm fine."

Anger joined the annoyance and... Dammit, knowing that he stayed up watching over her made her feel protected. Safe. She scratched her stinging wrist. She needed him to rest for a bit.

"You're no good to me if you're overtired, especially if we hit trouble in Bluefields."

She wondered who took care of this grumpy loner? Who bullied him into sleeping and resting and smiling sometimes?

"I'm fine. I've stayed up far longer than this."

When he was in the military. She kept glaring at him as they hiked on a bit farther. When he stopped again, she saw another clearing, but this one was silent.

She peered over Shep's shoulder, her gaze falling on a two-story wooden structure. It looked like a half-built hut, built up on stilts. There was no one around.

"It's abandoned," he said.

"I think we should stop here for a rest."

His eyebrows drew together. "Hayden—"

"My wrist is actually really hurting. From the ropes that those guys used to tie me up."

His frown deepened and he grabbed her arm. He shoved her sleeve up, then hissed out a breath. "Dammit, Hayden, this is infected. You should've told me."

"I didn't think it was too bad. I figured we were almost at Bluefields. But it is really hurting now."

"It needs antiseptic cream and a bandage."

An idea hit. "I'll make you a deal. I'll let you take care of this, *if* you rest and sleep for a bit."

The look he sent her was thunderous. "You're not in charge here."

She crossed her arms. "Then I guess we'll keep hiking to Bluefields."

He muttered something under his breath, then swiveled and moved over to the ladder leading up into the hut.

As he climbed up, Hayden smiled.

The inside of the structure was completely empty. There were several cut outs for windows, but no glass in them. Hayden sat down on the wooden floor and leaned back against the wall. Shep sat beside her.

He opened his backpack and pulled out a small first-aid kit.

"Show me," he ordered.

She held her wrist out. He made another unhappy sound, then spread some cream over it. He grabbed a bandage and wrapped it around her wrist before he secured it.

She was surprised at how gentle his touch was.

"Now you take a power nap," she said. "I'll stand guard."

He cocked a brow.

She waved for his handgun. "I can use it. My Secret Service people showed me how."

"Just ten minutes."

"Twenty," she counted.

His mouth flattened. "You are so stubborn."

"Not as stubborn as you are."

They glared at each other for a beat, then he handed over the gun, and muttered under his breath. "Fifteen minutes. Wake me if you see or hear anything."

She nodded, then watched as he leaned back against

the wall. Of course, the stubborn grump wasn't going to lie down.

But surprisingly, he dropped off to sleep fast.

Wow. She wished she could do that. She normally needed to read for at least thirty minutes before she could calm her mind down enough to fall asleep.

She looked out the window. It was all quiet outside, except for the birds in the trees.

The minutes ticked by, then Shep made a low sound. She glanced back in his direction and noted that he was still asleep, but his brow was creased.

What weight did he carry? What nightmares still haunted him?

"*No.* Jenny." His face twisted with grief.

Hayden froze. So much pain. He *had* lost someone.

Jenny.

Conflicted emotions hit her, but most of all she didn't want him suffering through a nightmare. She went to move closer and wake him, but he settled, his body relaxing again.

A second later, his eyes opened. He looked wide awake and alert.

"How do you do that?" she asked.

"What?"

"Fall asleep so fast and wake up so fast."

"Learned it in the military. In special forces you learn to take a nap whenever and wherever you can." He took the gun from her. "Everything okay?"

She nodded and rose, dusting off her trousers. "Who's Jenny?"

His body went rigid. He looked away, and she stared at the tight line of his jaw.

Damn her curiosity. She'd clearly dredged up something he didn't want to discuss.

"Sorry. Not my business. You said her name in your sleep. She's clearly important to you."

He dragged in a ragged breath, and then Hayden felt really horrible. This was clearly painful for him.

"Shep, I'm sorry."

He shrugged on his backpack.

"Jenny was my sister." Then he headed for the ladder. "Let's go." He disappeared.

Hayden cursed herself. *Was* his sister. That couldn't be good.

She followed him out of the hut.

CROUCHED IN THE BUSHES, Shep studied the two houses nestled near the road. They were little more than shacks. He spotted a dog wandering around.

He pressed his fingers to his lips and grabbed Hayden's hand. He pulled her quietly into the trees.

They'd come across more houses the closer they got to Bluefields.

Bluefields was the capital of the South Caribbean Autonomous Region in Nicaragua, but wasn't very big. It was the chief Caribbean port for the area, exporting hardwood and seafood.

The sun was out, and the jungle had turned steamy. Shep's shirt stuck to his back. Hayden looked even more bedraggled. No one would recognize her as the president's daughter.

When they were far enough from the houses, he pulled out his sat phone.

It was time to call for help. He held it to his ear and the call connected.

"Lancelot." It was Vander's voice saying Shep's codename.

"Yeah. I have your Christmas gift. I was planning to send it, but the plane had trouble."

"I heard. I was worried you were on it. The gift is undamaged?"

Shep glanced at Hayden. "Yeah, but we could do with some assistance."

"That can be arranged. I'm guessing you're feeling blue."

Feeling blue. Bluefields. "Yes. We are."

"I'll call you back." Vander ended the call.

"What was all that?" Hayden asked.

"I told Vander that you're safe, and we need extraction."

"Vander?" she said. "Vander Norcross?"

"You know him?"

"I've heard of him. Anyone who mentions his name always looks nervous. My father included."

"He was my commander. We butted heads a few times, but he's the first man I'd pick to cover my six." The phone vibrated and he answered the call. "Go."

"The Peralta Café. Three. The weather's hot today, so stay in the shade." Vander was gone.

"The Peralta Café."

Hayden straightened. "I know it. Some of the researchers from the dig went there. It has tasty local food."

"We need to be there at three o'clock." He checked his watch. "We can't be seen. Your kidnappers are looking for you."

Her nose wrinkled. "Great."

They set off again, walking parallel to a road, but staying in the trees. Shep wondered who Vander would send to pick them up.

"You must've gone on some dangerous missions," Hayden said.

"Yeah." His gut clenched. Too many to count. He cleared his throat. "Some were in the jungle, but most were in desert conditions."

"Afghanistan."

"I spent more time there than I wanted to."

"Thank you."

He frowned at her. "For what?"

"For your service. For doing a hard, dangerous job, so most people never have to know what that's like."

He looked at her for a beat, then nodded.

"I understand why you'd want to hide at your cabin in the mountains."

"I'm not hiding," he growled.

She touched a hand to his arm.

Just a simple touch, but he felt it, and her understanding all the way to his gut.

But more than that, this was Hayden's touch. His gut tightened, as did other parts of him. He knew exactly how it felt to have her hands on him, sliding down his gut and stroking his cock.

Shit. That had been a one-time deal they'd both agreed to never mention again.

He shook his head, trying to focus. "It sucked. It was hard. People shot at me, and I witnessed terrible atrocities. I killed." He dragged in a harsh breath. "And I saw good men die."

Because he hadn't reached them in time. Just like his little sister.

"Shep? Hey?"

A warm hand touched his cheek, and he jerked.

Brown eyes were steady on his. "I'm sorry I took you back there."

He jerked away. "Let's just keep moving." He turned and set off at a quick pace.

Soon, more buildings appeared, and there was more traffic on the road. The air now held a tang of salt. They reached an area with more buildings sat clumped closely together, all painted in bright colors. He stopped at the corner of a dilapidated building, and pulled Hayden close beside him.

The Peralta Café was across the road.

The building wasn't fancy, and was painted a bright blue. A rusted, tin roof covered the café, and a patio with columns lined the front of it.

Several cars drove past. There were a few tables outside, with one occupied by a couple.

"How do we know who our contact is?" she asked.

"They'll give us a sign."

The minutes ticked passed. Shep looked at his watch. Their contact was late.

"Maybe they're waiting to see us?" she suggested.

Maybe, but Shep didn't want to expose Hayden.

But it didn't look like he had a choice.

"Shit." He rose. "Come on. Stay close."

Side-by-side, they crossed the road. He scanned the area carefully. No one appeared to be paying them any extra attention.

The café had three tables outside, and they sat at one that was shielded by a potted plant in a bright-yellow pot. Across from him, Hayden fidgeted.

"Relax," he told her.

She rolled her eyes. "How do you suggest I do that?"

He leaned closer. "I could kiss you again."

Her gaze locked on his, and he felt that zing of attraction pass between them. Of all the people for him to be attracted to...

A powerful-sounding engine rumbled nearby. Glancing at the road, he saw a Mercedes SUV driving toward them, looking very shiny and out of place. It pulled to a stop in front of the café, and the driver's-side door opened.

The driver was a handsome man in his early thirties, wearing suit pants and a white-linen shirt. He had thick, black hair and a trimmed goatee. When he spotted them, he smiled.

A waitress leaned in. "Be careful of that one. He's all flash and all trouble."

Shep's instincts tingled. "Drug dealer?"

The woman nodded, then hurried inside.

CHAPTER NINE

Hayden's nerves stretched tight as she watched the man stroll their way. He was well dressed, with a wide smile.

"He's a drug dealer?" she whispered. "Are we sure this is a good idea?"

"We have to trust Vander." But Shep was frowning hard.

"My friends." The man spread his arms wide like they'd known each other their entire lives.

"Name?" Shep said sharply.

"You Americans, always so direct." He turned a chair around and sat, crossing his arms over the back's top. Then he waved a hand at the waitress hovering near the doorway. He spoke in rapid-fire Spanish, and shot her a charming smile.

She sniffed, then went back inside.

His dark gaze settled back on Shep and Hayden. "My name is Miguel. I'm a friend of our mutual dark-haired *amigo* from San Franciso."

Hayden saw a muscle tick in Shep's jaw.

Miguel leaned forward. "I hope you get to enjoy our lovely city." His dark gaze flicked to Hayden. "Did you know Bluefields is named after the Dutch-Jewish pirate Abraham Blauvelt? They also named a town in Jamaica after him as well." Miguel waved a hand. "It can get confusing."

"You're a drug trafficker," Shep said.

Miguel's face sharpened, and Hayden saw intelligence in his eyes. His charming demeanor was just a cover. It would pay not to underestimate the man.

"I'm a businessman." Miguel spread his hands. "We are a poor nation, and we do what we have to do to survive. My country is a go-between from South and North America." He shrugged. "But my profession has nothing to do with you. Vander Norcross saved my life once, and I owe him." The charming smile reappeared. "Bluefields is a charming mix of religions and ethnic groups. We have our native Miskitos, Creoles, and Mestizo, who are of mixed European and indigenous ancestry, like myself. And while Spanish is my country's official language, here on the Caribbean coast, we also speak Creole English."

"We don't need a history lesson or a tour guide," Shep said.

"I know, but you do need some help. I suggest we leave quickly." Miguel's dark gaze flicked to Hayden. "There are many people looking for the beautiful Ms. Sinclair."

Hayden swallowed and glanced at Shep.

His face looked like a thundercloud. She could tell he

wasn't happy about the situation. But they didn't really have a choice.

"What's the plan?" Shep asked.

"It's best not to discuss it here." Miguel smiled. "I'll take you somewhere safe. Where I also have clean clothes." He eyed their rumpled clothes with distaste. "And food, and a place to rest until Vander makes contact. He is arranging travel out of the country for you." Miguel gave an elegant shrug. "The airport is not a good option."

That wasn't good. She saw that muscle tick in Shep's jaw again.

The waitress bought an espresso and set it in front of Miguel. The man smiled and drank it in one gulp. He threw some cash on the table. "So, my friends?"

Shep nodded. He took Hayden's hand, and they rose.

Suddenly, Shep stiffened. Miguel's smile evaporated, as well.

Three men were walking down the street toward the café. Their gazes were locked on Hayden.

Her stomach turned over. "Shep..."

"I see them. Don't worry, I've got this." Shep drew a handgun, keeping it down by his side.

"Time to move." Miguel's voice was deep, all charm gone. "I suggest we get to my vehicle."

In a smooth move, Miguel pulled out a gun and fired.

Screams broke out, and the three men on the road dove for cover. With a curse, Shep lifted his gun and fired as well. He yanked Hayden down, then knocked the table over on its side for cover. Glasses smashed on the pavement. Miguel slid in beside them.

"Friends of yours?" Shep asked.

"No." Miguel looked offended. "They are scum."

That sounded a bit rich coming from a drug dealer, but since he was helping them, Hayden was on his side.

"These men sell their services to the highest bidder."

Hayden's throat closed. More gunfire peppered the café. She threw her arms over her head.

"Miguel, give us cover fire." Shep peered at the vehicle. "I'll get Hayden to your SUV."

The drug dealer pulled a second handgun from his waistband and smiled back. He looked quite happy with the situation. "My pleasure, *amigo*."

Miguel rose and fired both guns.

"*Run.*" Shep dragged her out of cover, firing his weapon. They sprinted, hunched over, racing off the patio toward the SUV.

Bullets ripped up tables. A scream lodged in Hayden's throat, but she just focused on the vehicle. Adrenaline left her feeling jittery and amped up.

They reached the vehicle, and Shep ripped the back door open. He shoved her inside and she scrambled in.

There was more gunfire. Bullets pinged off the SUV, and Shep returned fire.

A second later, the driver's side door opened, and Miguel threw himself inside.

"Good shooting, my friend. Now, get in."

Shep had barely gotten in the SUV, the door still open, when Miguel stepped on the gas.

The SUV roared down the street. A car swerved to avoid them, honking its horn. Shep slammed the door closed. Hayden quickly fastened her seatbelt.

Miguel laughed. "That was fun. You're a good shot... you didn't tell me your name."

Shep looked reluctant. "It's Shep."

"Shep. So very American."

Miguel took a corner too fast, and Hayden braced a hand on the door.

"I need to ensure our friends back there don't follow us. Unfortunately, word has gotten around that Ms. Sinclair was spotted."

"Fuck," Shep muttered.

They turned another corner and this time Hayden slammed into Shep. He slid an arm across her shoulders to steady her.

"Do not worry," Miguel said. "I grew up here, so I know these roads well. I will take you to a house I've prepared for you. It's on the ocean and very secluded. No one will find you there. Plus, it has excellent security. I have enemies, you know."

Hayden just wanted to get home. Her pulse was racing, and her chest was tight. She glanced out the back window. Thankfully, no one appeared to be following them.

"Ms. Sinclair, I'm sure a hot shower, clean clothes, and a meal will make you feel much better." Miguel met her gaze in the rearview mirror. "There is also a lovely pool. Try to enjoy yourself the best you can until our friend Vander gets you home."

She was pretty sure she wouldn't be relaxing anytime soon. "Thanks, Miguel."

SHEP STARED out the window as the tires crunched on the sandy driveway. Miguel drove them through a stand of palm trees. The drug dealer had driven a long and winding path around the area to ensure no one was tailing them.

"No one knows I own this house." Miguel tapped his fingers on the wheel. "I only use it when...I need to get away from things. Or when friends need a place to stay."

Shep's gaze sharpened on the man. "You have a lot of friends on the run who stop by?"

Miguel flashed a smile. "A few."

Shep realized there was more to the man than he'd originally thought. "You're CIA."

Miguel met his gaze in the rearview mirror. "I'm simply a man trying to make a living. You probably know better than anyone that no one is all black or white."

Shep snorted. "I think some people hide a lot of secrets under their flashy façade."

"Façade? *Amigo*, you wound me."

They rounded a bend, and the bay came into view. Water lapped at the shoreline. There was no beach—the beaches were on the other side of the bay.

Then, he saw the house.

It wasn't big or fancy, which made him like it more. It was a wooden house, with a large verandah facing the water. A kidney-shaped pool sat between the house and the water, surrounded by colorful bougainvillea flowers and palm trees.

And best of all, the place was secluded.

Miguel stopped the vehicle. "The house has every-thing you need." He turned in his seat and met Shep's gaze. "Everything. The windows have security bars, and the security system is very good. I installed it myself. There is also a locked cabinet in the living area under the television. It has provisions. The code is 7318."

Weapons. Shep nodded and held out a hand. "Thanks."

Miguel shook it. "Lay low, my friends. Lovely Ms. Sinclair, good luck." He took her hand and kissed it, which made Shep scowl.

"Thanks again, Miguel," she said.

Once they climbed out, they watched the SUV drive away. Shep headed up the steps.

"This is lovely," Hayden said, drawing in a deep breath.

He pushed open the door. The place had wooden floors and high ceilings. It had an airy, vacation-escape vibe. There was a modern kitchen, and one bedroom, the bed draped in a gauzy mosquito net.

Hayden looked around. "Vander sure came through."

"He always does. Go. Take a shower. There should be clean clothes in the closet."

With a smile, she headed for the bedroom and closed the door.

Shep strode to the front picture window and glanced around. Nothing but squawking birds, flourishing vegetation, and the gleaming water of the pool.

But he felt edgy. He hated being trapped and forced to wait. He preferred action.

He wanted to get Hayden out of the country and safe.

What he didn't want to do was sit still and wait, no matter how pretty the location.

He heard the shower start running. *Fuck.* He rubbed his forehead. Now he was thinking about Hayden— naked and wet.

With a curse, he headed out onto the veranda. A breeze blew in off the bay, but it did little to cool him off.

Dammit. He needed to focus on his job—keeping the president's daughter safe and getting her out of here in one piece.

He stomped back inside. He noted the delicate bars on the windows which he guessed were reinforced. The doors were also all wired and had extra secure locks. He ignored the running shower and found the locked cabinet under the TV. He entered the code and it opened with a hiss.

Nice. Now he smiled.

A collection of weapons was nestled inside. There was also a laptop.

He sat on the couch, set the computer on the coffee table, and opened it. Unsurprisingly, the house had satellite Internet. The first thing he did was check the security systems.

Several security feeds filled the screen, along with the status of all the sensors—interior and exterior.

It was good. "Well done, Miguel," he muttered under his breath. No one could sneak up on them without setting off the alarm. He quickly sent a message to Vander.

A second later, a video call chimed, and he answered it.

Vander's face filled the screen.

"Shep. You all right?"

"Still breathing, and no new bullet holes."

Vander nodded. "Hayden?"

"She's fine. Miguel came through. Thanks for that."

"You need to lay low. Bluefields is hot, and since Miguel didn't exactly pick you up quietly, the word is out that Hayden is there."

"*Fuck.*" Shep glanced at the closed bedroom door.

"She's holding up okay?"

"Yeah. She's not what I expected."

"Do I hear grudging respect from the extremely hard-to-please Shepherd Barlow?"

Shep ignored his friend. "Exit plan?"

"I'm working on it. The plan is to send a jet, but you'd have to run a gauntlet to get to the airport."

Dammit. Not what he wanted to do. It would put Hayden at too much risk.

"What about a water option?"

"That'll take time." Vander paused. "And I have more bad news."

Great.

"An Iranian team touched down in Nicaragua."

Shep stiffened. "What?"

"Four of them. All Quds."

"Fucking hell." The Quds Force was a branch of Iran's Islamic Revolutionary Guard Corps, specializing in unconventional warfare and military intelligence. It was equivalent to the CIA, with a dash of special forces.

"They want her badly, Shep. They were one of the most interested buyers her abductors had lined up."

Shep's fingers curled into his palm. "Well, they can't have her."

The bedroom door opened. Hayden came out wearing cut-off denim shorts, and a black tank. There was a black tie around her neck, which made him guess she was wearing a swimsuit underneath. He fought not to look at her legs. Her wet hair was shades darker than normal, and her face was clean and fresh.

"Who are you talking to?" she asked.

"Vander."

She moved behind the couch, leaning over Shep's shoulder. He felt her breasts brush his back and he stifled a groan.

"Ms. Sinclair, how are you?" Vander asked.

"I'm good, considering. It's nice to meet you, Vander. And please call me Hayden."

"I hope Shep is taking good care of you."

She snorted. "He is, in his annoying, overbearing way."

Shep scowled, and watched Vander fighting a smile.

"That sounds like Shep."

She pressed a hand to his shoulder. "I'm alive, thanks to him."

Vander nodded. "There's no one I trust more. Lay low for now. Once we have your extraction ready, I'll be in touch." He nodded, and the screen went black.

"What did he *not* say in front of me?" she asked.

Shep looked up at her. Her lips were pressed together, forming lines around her mouth, but her gaze was steady. This woman was strong. She took whatever life threw at her, and dealt with it.

"A team of Iranian special forces touched down in the country. They're highly skilled."

She blew out a breath. "That's just great. I take it they want to take me on a trip?"

He took her hand. "They're *not* getting close enough to sniff you."

She gave a startled laugh. "At least I smell better after that hot shower. You, on the other hand..."

Shep rose. "I'll shower now."

"Is it okay to go outside?"

"Yes, but take this." He held out a handgun from Miguel's stash. "Do you know how to use it?"

She nodded. "Maria taught me." Grief crossed her face.

He gripped her shoulder and gave it a quick squeeze. "Stay close to the house. No one knows we're here, but..."

"I'm being hunted down like I'm not even human."

"Hey." He waited until she met his gaze. "Anyone coming for you has to go through me first. Don't forget that."

CHAPTER TEN

Hayden wandered aimlessly around the pool. She felt edgy and restless. She couldn't appreciate the scent of the flowers, or the warmth of the sun.

She was thinking of Maria. Thinking of what would happen if the bad guys got her. She kicked an outdoor chair, and it skidded across the paving. She was so angry and scared and sad.

She squeezed her eyes closed. The truth was, she might not make it out of here.

If she was caught, they'd use her against her father, against her country. They'd hurt her, and possibly kill her.

Blowing out a breath, she tipped her face to the sky. Shep would risk his life for her. Because that was the kind of guy he was.

A damn hero hiding under a grumpy exterior.

She needed to burn off some energy. She looked around and her gaze settled on the pool.

She was wearing a bikini under her shorts and T-shirt. She'd hand-washed her underwear, but she'd found no new underwear in the clothing stash. She had, however, found a black bikini.

Perfect. She stripped her clothes off and tossed them on a chair. She'd swim a few laps until she was too tired to think and worry.

The bikini was on the small side, barely holding her breasts in place, but thankfully no one was around.

She walked into the pool, the water warm against her skin, then dived underneath the surface. She started swimming laps. She'd been on the swim team through high school and college, and her body easily fell into the familiar rhythm. The pool wasn't really long enough, but it would do. As she did a few laps, she felt herself settle.

When she finally stopped and stood, she sensed someone watching her.

Shep stood by the edge of the pool, hands in the pockets of a pair of brown cargo shorts. Everything inside of her stilled. He was so big and solid. The clean, black T-shirt he wore clung to his chest, the sleeves digging into his muscular biceps. She swallowed. His dark hair was damp, and his black beard trimmed.

Desire hit her full force.

She wanted him, plain and simple.

Of course, he was scowling at her, but she kind of liked his scowls now.

"What are you wearing?" His tone was all grit and growl.

"A bikini. It's all I could find inside for underwear, but it might surprise you to know that it's commonly worn by women when they go in a swimming pool."

His gaze dropped, and she felt it on her body like a physical touch. Heat coiled low in her belly. She remembered exactly how it felt when he touched her. Remembered how it felt when those strong, calloused fingers rubbed her clit and made her come.

Then he looked over her shoulder and his scowl deepened.

Hayden licked her lips. She didn't want a relationship, and Shep didn't, either. They'd been thrown together in dangerous circumstances. Circumstances they might not survive.

She let her gaze travel over those muscular arms. Strong arms that had kept her safe.

She might not want a relationship, but right now, she wanted Shep. Making the decision, she strode to the steps and walked out of the pool. His gaze was like a hot brand on her skin, and she fought not to shiver.

She stopped in front of him. "We're safe here, right?"

"For the moment."

"But getting out of Nicaragua is going to be dangerous."

He didn't answer, but kept his gaze locked on hers.

"We might not make it," she murmured.

"I'm going to get you out."

"You can't guarantee that." She pressed a hand to his rock-hard chest. She wanted to see what it looked like with no shirt.

"Go inside and get dressed," he said.

She shook her head.

The groove in his brow deepened. "Hayden."

She reached back and unfastened the bikini top. It hit the paving with a wet slap.

His jaw locked. "Hayden, what the—?"

"I want you, Shep. I want to fuck you. I want to explore your body." She pulled in a breath and took a step closer. "I want to forget everything for a while. Just enjoy...being close to someone. Being close to you."

She saw so much emotion swirling in his green eyes. He was waging an internal battle.

God, what if he wasn't as attracted as she was?

"It doesn't have to mean anything," she hurried on. "I'm not asking for a ring or commitment. I don't want those things. You don't want those things."

He still didn't move.

Maybe he didn't want her. Embarrassment, hot and acute, crawled up her throat. "Forget it." She started to step back.

A brawny arm wrapped around her, hauling her up against him. Her bare breasts pressed against his chest, and she gasped. Her nipples were hard points, and she could feel heat pumping off him.

"It can be casual, Hayden, but it'll still mean something."

Her pulse went haywire.

Then he lowered his head and kissed her.

Oh, God.

His tongue pushed into her mouth, hot and demanding. She wrapped her arms around him and kissed him back.

"Tried to fight this." He bit her bottom lip. "Shouldn't be touching you."

"Shut up and kiss me."

The kiss was wild, fueled by mutual need. They were both trying to take control. Shep's conversation skills might be lacking, his kissing skills were not.

His fingers slid into her hair, holding her in place for the assault by his mouth. She moaned, waves of excitement and desire pumping through her. She hadn't expected the hunger or the intensity. She felt a rush of damp between her thighs, and she rocked against him.

One big palm cupped her ass and pushed. She leaped up and wrapped her legs around his waist. His mouth moved over hers and she opened wider, her fingers digging into his shoulders.

"I can make you forget everything," he murmured against her lips. "Everything but me."

Then he turned and carried her inside.

SHEP HAD FELT DESIRE BEFORE.

Desire was easy. An itch to be scratched, then forgotten.

But this pounding, hungry need clawing at him, he had no idea what it was.

"We need...rules," Hayden panted.

Her face was flushed, her hair wet. Those beautiful breasts—not too big and not too small—bobbed as he carried her.

"No rules," he growled.

He kicked the door open, and at least had enough brain cells still functioning to close and lock it.

He shouldn't be touching her. They were safe for now, but he was her protection. She was the president's daughter. He didn't want to get close to someone.

He had lots of damn reasons to keep his hands off Hayden Sinclair.

But he couldn't stop.

"No rules," he said again, "just fucking."

She licked her lips. "I can get behind that."

He pressed his mouth to her neck and sucked. He felt her racing pulse fluttering there. "Oh, I'm going to be behind you, beautiful." He raked his teeth over her skin.

Her breath hitched.

The only things echoing in Shep's head were the pounding need to make her come, followed by the need to sink his cock inside her.

But first, those breasts topped with cherry-red nipples were taunting him.

He'd barely touched her, and his cock was harder than it had ever been. The need stronger than it had ever been.

He made a hungry sound, then sucked one nipple into his mouth. She cried out his name, her hands spearing into his hair. That tight body rubbed against him.

His mouth came off her nipple with a pop. "You wet for me, Hayden?"

"God, I can barely get you to say a full sentence, but get naked in front of you, and you have all kinds of dirty things to say."

"And you clearly like it." He laughed, then moved to her other nipple. He blew on it.

As she moaned, her gaze met his, hot and burning. "I do like it. Men usually treat me like a perfect, boring..."

"Lady?" He closed the distance to the back of the couch, then rested her ass on the back. He nudged her legs apart. The tiny, string-bikini bottoms didn't hide much. "Don't worry." He slid his hands up her thighs. "I'll treat you dirty, beautiful." God, he loved seeing his tanned hands against her pale thighs.

She pulled his head down, and bit his bottom lip. "I want rough, Shep. Hard."

He growled, rubbing his fingers between her legs. She was soaked. He shoved the fabric aside, stroking her slick flesh.

Hayden cried out.

He liked that sound. "So damn wet. All for me." He pressed his fingers inside her, and she made a garbled sound.

Shep never left a bed partner unsatisfied, but he'd never felt so driven to make a woman come. Never wanted to watch her face while she found her pleasure. The pleasure he gave her.

He found her clit, working it with his thumb. Her body jerked.

"Yes, Shep, *God*..."

He pressed his mouth to her jaw. "You smell like flowers."

"From the shower," she panted.

The sweet scent clung to her skin. He pumped his fingers inside her, and the air rushed out of her, fast and ragged.

He took her mouth with his. He needed it. She kissed

him back with tongue and teeth. He pushed another finger inside her. Damn, she was tight. His cock throbbed as he imagined how that sweet pussy would feel around him.

"*Hurry.*" Her hips jerked.

"I'm in charge here."

Her lips parted. "It hurts. Make me come, Shep." Her hands slid into his hair and tugged hard. "*Please.*" The word was a snarl.

He wanted to soothe away her hurts. *Fuck.* He'd never soothed anyone in his life.

But he could make this beautiful woman come.

"You're so tight, Hayden. I can't wait to slide my cock in here. You'll feel me."

Her body shook.

Using her slick juices, he circled her clit, rubbing harder. His fingers filled her as he kept pumping them inside her.

"You come for me now, beautiful. Ride my fingers. Next time, you'll come on my cock."

Her climax hit, and a cry broke from her. Her back arched. "*Shep!*"

Damn. He'd never seen anything so beautiful. He slid an arm around her to stop her sliding off the back of the couch. She was breathing heavily, her body shaking as the pleasure swamped her.

"You're so damn beautiful, Hayden."

There was a faint flush of pink in her cheeks. He'd never told a woman she was beautiful before. Especially not when she was naked in his arms.

"Take your shirt off," she demanded, voice husky.

He grabbed the back of his shirt and ripped it over his head.

Her eyes flashed. "You don't look real." She stroked his chest, running her fingers through the faint smattering of dark hair across his pecs. Then her fingers moved down his abs, tracing over the heavy ridges.

Seeing the flush on her face made him damn glad he worked out so much. "I'm real. As real as the orgasm you just had."

"And I want more." She paused a few times when she found one of his scars. She traced a finger down the ragged line on his side. "This must have hurt."

"Knife wound. Healed up all right."

Her fingers drifted lower and circled two round puckered scars. He tensed.

But she didn't linger long and didn't ask any questions. Just faint caresses, like she was trying to ease away those old hurts. Then she pressed a kiss to the center of his chest.

"You have a warrior's body, Shep." Her hand moved lower. "Big, strong, scarred..." Her hand pressed against the front of his shorts, palming his rock-hard cock.

He couldn't stop the low groan that escaped him.

"Did I mention big?" Her voice was breathless. "I want you inside me, Shep. *Now*."

CHAPTER ELEVEN

Hayden was still trying to recover from her orgasm.

Her amazing, earth-shattering orgasm.

Shep's big chest was rising and falling. The raw need on his face made her muscles lock. Desire throbbed off him, and the tendons in his neck strained.

Under her palm, she felt the throb of his swollen cock. God, she needed him so badly. Needed that big body on hers, in hers...

His hands gripped her thighs and her pulse jumped.

"I want my mouth on your pussy," he growled.

Her belly clenched. "Later. Please, Shep, I need you inside me."

White-hot desire was growing in her belly, coiling tight. More than anything, she needed the big cock she felt pushing hard against his zipper.

She grabbed the waistband of his shorts and flicked open the top button.

He pushed her hands away and quickly shucked the shorts.

Oh. He was commando underneath. Her heart beat hard in her chest. Like the rest of his carved body, his cock was big, long, and hard. There was a bead of pre-come at the tip.

"Come inside me." She felt a flush of heat over her skin, and she burned inside as well.

He made a deep, masculine sound. Almost pained. Then he gripped her hips and flipped her over.

Hayden gasped, finding herself bent over the back of the couch, her toes barely touching the floor.

A callused hand pressed against her spine, then she felt hot lips on the back of her neck.

"You want my cock? Well, you're getting it." He bit her earlobe. "Think you can handle it?"

"*Yes.*" She pushed back against him and felt the head of his cock rub against her ass.

Shep groaned and gripped her hips. "Fuck, Hayden..." He notched himself between her thighs, then surged forward.

She cried out. The powerful thrust sent the couch sliding across the floor.

"Damn, you're tight." His voice was a low growl.

She closed her eyes and breathed through the almost unbearable pleasure. She felt stretched, full, taken.

"Look at you." His fingers clenched on her skin. "Look at how you take me."

"Shep, *move.*" Her fingers dug into the couch.

He pulled out and thrust back inside. She cried out his name.

"That's it, beautiful. Take it. Take me."

As he slammed inside her, she rocked into his thrusts. She bit her lip. She'd never felt this taken, this possessed.

He pressed his sweat-slicked chest to her back. She felt the flex of his muscles as he fucked her. The man fucked like a powerhouse.

She turned her head, and he bent over her, his mouth touching hers.

"Feel good?"

"Yes," she panted.

Then she felt his hand beneath her, and he found her clit. She bit her lip as he stroked her.

His thrusts got faster, harder.

"I want you to come all over my cock, Hayden."

Everything inside her contracted. This was the hottest, sexiest moment of her life. It wasn't careful or polite or delicate. No, it was hard and hot and breathless.

"I need it," she whispered. "Fuck me, Shep."

His next thrust was savage, and he pinched her clit.

"God. *Oh*—" Her voice broke as her orgasm hit her in a blinding flash. Her pussy clenched on the big invader inside her, pleasure spasming through her. She screamed his name.

"Hayden, *fuck*." On his next thrust he buried himself deep inside her.

She heard his groan, and felt the pulse of heat inside her. His fingers clenched on her hips hard enough to bruise. She loved hearing him find his own climax.

They both collapsed on the back of the couch, bodies convulsing with pleasure. His big body pinned her down.

Hayden felt safe. Well used, wrecked, and safe. She swallowed.

Safe wasn't something she was used to feeling. She was so used to being on guard, and questioning other people's motives, that it was habit. The Dillon debacle hadn't helped one bit.

But with big, grumpy, protective Shep, she could just...be.

She felt his heart beating against her back. She wanted to kiss him, and wring a smile from that hard mouth. She wanted to touch him and run her hands through his dark hair. To let him relax, and not carry all that weight she saw in his eyes.

But she didn't move. This was just a casual fuck between two almost-strangers in terrible circumstances. She curled her fingers into her palms. She couldn't let herself forget that.

Shep shifted, and another lazy shot of pleasure moved through her body. That's when she realized his cock was still hard and thick inside her.

"Not done yet," he growled against her ear.

She swallowed, her pulse tripping. "Okay."

———

AS SHEP PULLED out of Hayden, he heard her soft moan.

He closed his eyes, and savored the sensation. Before he thought about it, he kissed the center of her back.

Shit. What the hell was he doing? He wasn't a snuggler, or a man who liked any sort of affection. He didn't hold hands or give gentle kisses.

He straightened and pulled her upright.

The look on her face... His gut clenched. Her cheeks were flushed, her mouth swollen. Her face reflected bliss. She looked very-well-fucked.

And he'd never seen a woman look more beautiful.

His gaze slid down her body. A body he wanted to explore. He noted their mixed release trickling down her thigh, and he tensed.

Oh, hell. He cleared his throat. "I... We didn't use protection."

It was stupid. In the moment, he hadn't even thought about it. That had never happened before.

She cleared her throat. "I had a physical before I came down to the dig. I'm healthy. And I had a contraceptive shot, as well. So, it's fine. You?"

Trying not to think about the fact that his come was leaking down her thigh, he cleared his throat. "I'm clean. I haven't been with anyone for a while."

She gave him a faint smile. "Because you stay up on your mountain? Alone and brooding?"

He narrowed his gaze. "Something like that."

"Writing sad poetry."

She was teasing him. No one did that except his buddies. "Avoiding annoying people." He scooped her up and tossed over his shoulder. "Like a certain blonde who doesn't know when to be quiet."

"Shep!"

"Avoiding annoying, sexy women who clearly need to be taught a lesson." He slapped a palm against her ass.

She laughed.

She had a good one. And he knew she needed the laughter after the last few days.

He stopped in the bathroom and set her on the vanity.

She blinked. "What are—?"

He took a cloth and turned on the faucet, wetting the fabric. He wrung the water out, then wiped between her legs. She let out a low gasp as he gently cleaned her.

Taking care of a woman like this wasn't something he'd done before, but he just followed his instincts. Her lips parted, and soon she was squirming. He fought a smile. His sexy archeologist was turned on again.

Or maybe still turned on. His cock was still hard and wanted back inside her.

But not before he got his mouth on that sweet pussy first. He tossed the cloth in the sink and scooped her up again.

"Shep—"

He kissed her. He couldn't stop himself. She had a mouth made for kissing.

She clung to him, hand pressed to the side of his head as she moaned against his lips.

He carried her into the bedroom. She barely took note of him shoving the mosquito net hanging over the bed aside, her mouth busy on his. He laid her down on the mattress.

Damn, she was so beautiful. She had a fit body that he really liked. A neat strip of dark blonde hair between her legs. A nipped in waist and breasts he wanted to get better acquainted with.

The net fell back into place, separating them. It made everything seem like a hazy dream. He pushed it up enough to bare her legs. Then he reached the juncture of her thighs.

He stroked her swollen flesh. "Every bit of you is beautiful."

She writhed and he liked that. He leaned down and bit her inner thigh. She jerked and gasped.

"If you want my mouth, hold still," he ordered.

"Just do it," she panted.

"You don't get to give orders." Their gazes met through the netting.

Her stubborn chin jutted. "We'll see."

He bit her again, and clamped his hands on her soft flesh. Then he pressed his mouth to her pussy.

She cried out and reared up, but he held her down.

He'd known she'd be sweet and spicy.

He took his time, lapping and sucking. It didn't take him long to work out that she preferred her clit sucked, while he slid a finger inside her.

Her husky cries made him work harder. God, she was perfect. Her hips thrust up against his mouth, while he ground his hips against the mattress. His cock was weeping and painfully hard.

Hayden sat up, yanking at the netting. "Come here."

"What do you need, princess?"

"*You.* That hard body and big cock." She tugged him toward her.

Shep fell onto his back beside her. She was on him in a flash. Her hands pressed to his chest, and she straddled him, her slick, hot pussy rubbing against his abs.

"I love your body," she panted.

"I prefer yours." He cupped one of her breasts. She

was the perfect blend of firm and soft. "I wasn't done eating you."

"I want a turn." She whirled, kneeling beside his hip on the bed. She took his cock in her hand.

A groan ripped out of him.

Before he could shore up his control, she lowered her head and sucked him into her warm mouth.

"*Hayden*. Fucking hell." His body locked.

She made a humming sound, getting off on blowing him. Knowing Hayden, driving him out of his mind turned her on.

She leaned over, sucking his cock, and gave him a perfect view of her ass.

With a growl, he gripped her thighs and yanked her closer.

"*Shep*." She shifted to keep her balance. He pulled her thighs either side of his head and licked her.

"*Oh*."

He found her swollen clit and sucked.

The sounds she made sent more blood to his cock. He wouldn't last much longer.

She recovered enough to suck his cock back into her mouth. It was almost a battle—fighting to give each other pleasure. Trying to drive the other past the edge of control and into mindless pleasure.

Shep had no plans to spill down her throat. He wanted inside her again. This time, he wanted a clear view of her face when she came.

He'd never wanted that before. As long as a partner came, he'd never felt the urge to watch them find it.

He didn't stop to think about it. He gripped Hayden's

waist and pushed her flat on her back. He covered her body with his.

"*Yes*," she breathed.

He gripped his cock and lined up. Then he pressed inside her.

She made a sound that he felt in his cock. With a groan, he threw his head back and pushed deeper. "So damn tight." Pleasure surged into his gut and up his spine.

Nothing existed except the two of them. He slid a hand between them to feel where she was split open and stretched by his cock.

"Shep, don't stop." Her voice was breathy.

Their gazes meshed.

He thrust harder, liking the way her breasts jiggled. "You look so good taking my cock."

In response, she moaned.

Shep picked up the pace, his hips snapping forward. He grunted, pleasure coiling around his spine. His vision dimmed. All that existed was this fierce need. All that existed was Hayden.

Strong but soft Hayden who gave as good as she got. Who didn't bend or break. Who he knew he could count on when things got tough.

"Yes, God, I'm coming!" Her nails scored his back.

He pulled back, and slammed forward as deep as he could go. Her pussy clenched on him.

"Damn, I want this all the fucking time." The words pushed between his clenched teeth. "This is mine."

She screamed his name. It ripped the release out of

him, and he groaned, a raw sound. His cock throbbed hard as they both came together.

He collapsed beside her, pulling her close. The only sound was their fast breathing, and the scent of sex wrapped around them. He slid a hand into her golden hair, cupping the back of her head.

"Shep." She pressed a kiss to his chest, and made a lazy sound. "That was..."

"Yeah. It was."

Shep pulled her closer and looked up at the netting above. An unfamiliar and uncomfortable tug in his chest made him frown. But he didn't let her go.

For the first time in his life, he'd found a person he liked being tangled with. Someone who, for the moment, made him not want to let go.

He wouldn't get to keep Hayden Sinclair, but for today, he was keeping her.

CHAPTER TWELVE

R esting on one elbow, Shep watched the rise and fall of Hayden's chest.

Shit. His own chest tightened. He'd never watched anyone sleep before.

She stirred and rolled onto her side. His gaze dropped to the sweet curve of her ass. He noted she had some stubble burn on her thighs, and the image made his cock twitch. He'd had a very pleasurable time putting those marks on her. In fact, he really liked seeing his marks on her.

He wanted her again. He'd already tired her out this afternoon, and he shouldn't need her again this soon. Besides, she needed the rest after everything she'd been through.

She'd probably wake up hungry. Maybe he should get her some food?

Rising, he walked naked to the kitchen. He took a second to check the security system. Everything was quiet, and there were no messages from Vander.

Crap. That meant they still had no solid exit plan.

But Vander would come through. He always did.

Shep checked the fridge. It was well-stocked, and there were also some cooked local dishes.

He saw *pan de coco*, bread made with coconut milk, and a rice and bean dish. There were also some *queques*, cakes made with banana. He loaded up a plate with some of all the food, then grabbed two bottles of water, then headed back into the bedroom.

He set the stuff down on the bedside table, then tied up the mosquito net. He set the plate on the bed.

Hayden woke up and rolled over with a smile. Damn, she was beautiful.

Her gaze ran down his chest. He had a few scratch marks courtesy of her nails. She lingered on his abs, before her gaze dropped to his half-hard cock. Then, her attention caught on the plate of food.

"What's this?"

"Food."

She rolled her eyes and propped herself up. "It looks good. You made it?"

"I plated it. There are a few local dishes in the fridge." He pointed to the plate. "That's *pan de coco*. Bread made with coconut milk."

She tried a bite, and moaned. "It's really good."

"Figured you'd be hungry." He handed her a bottle of water.

"We did burn off some calories. Look at you, so thoughtful and caring."

He grunted, and stuffed some food in his mouth. "We needed to eat."

When Hayden sat up, he couldn't not look at her breasts. Breasts he'd spent a long time worshiping.

"You know, after spending some time together—" she broke off another piece of bread "—I think under the gruff, grumpy personality, you're hiding a good guy."

"You're delusional."

"The grump is just a front."

"Nope. I've always been like this."

"Really? I bet you drove your mom and dad crazy."

He stilled. "There was no dad. He left when I was young. When my sister was just a baby."

Crap. The words just blurted out. He never talked about his family.

"I'm sorry," she said.

He shrugged a shoulder.

"So, it was just you, your mom, and Jenny?" Hayden said. "I always wanted a sister."

He felt like claws were sinking into his gut. "We moved in with my grandfather." Shep paused. "He wasn't a nice guy."

Her face fell. "Shep..."

"Mom was afraid of him, but she had nowhere else to go. He lost his temper a lot." Grandpa Barlow had liked to discipline Shep with his belt a lot, too.

"He was abusive?"

"He was old-school. And mean. I tried to keep his attention off mom and Jenny."

"*Shep.*" She moved closer.

"Don't touch me," he bit out.

She froze but lifted her chin. "He hit you."

Shep shrugged again. "As long as he didn't hit Jenny,

I was happy. She was tiny, delicate." He remembered her sweet laughter. And her tears when he'd be black-and-blue with bruises.

"Your mom didn't leave?"

"No." His hand flexed. "Like I said, we had nowhere to go."

Anger sparked in Hayden's eyes. "She didn't try to protect you?"

"She was afraid." But yeah, a part of him blamed her. "One day, she told me to go out with friends. That she'd stay with Jenny. Grandpa was extra ornery that day, but I really wanted to go." They'd been friends who played football, and he'd rarely had the chance to escape, to laugh and joke with his buddies.

He saw understanding bleed into Hayden's eyes. She moved closer, but didn't touch him, just slid her hand on the bed until her pinky finger was a whisper away from his.

"What happened?"

"I stayed out past curfew." He'd just wanted to feel normal for a change. "And I was too late. I left my little sister unprotected." He looked at the wall, his gut tight as a rock. "While I was out, my grandfather lost it. Threw Jenny against the wall. She suffered a traumatic brain injury, and never woke up."

He missed that sweet, little girl. He'd failed her. He'd been older, bigger, stronger, but it hadn't done any good.

"Screw this." Hayden crawled onto his lap. She clamped her arms and legs around him. "Tell me he went to jail."

Shep pulled in a breath, filling his senses with the

scent of her. "Yeah. He died a few years later in a prison fight."

"Good." She hugged him. "I'm so sorry, Shep. I'm so sorry you lost your Jenny."

A shudder ran through him, then he hugged her back.

After a quiet moment, she asked, "What happened to your mom?"

"Not sure." Acid burned in his throat. "When I was old enough to enlist, I joined the Army. I never went back. I heard she remarried."

Hayden's hands stroked over his back.

"It's a trait of mine—" his voice was gruff "—to be too late to save the people who matter."

"Shep, it was *not* your fault. Your grandfather was to blame." Her lips pressed to his temple. "You were a kid. I bet Jenny wouldn't blame you. She'd be mad if you did."

"It wasn't the only time," he said, voice a monotone.

Hayden stilled. "You're talking about the friends you lost in Afghanistan."

He gritted his teeth, glad she couldn't see his face. "Yeah. I lost them in the worst possible way. Vander and I, and the rest of our team worked hard to find them."

She held him tighter.

"But I was too fucking late. They were waiting for us to find them, but three of them had been tortured and beheaded. The Taliban were about to kill Boone, too. We got him out, but the others died in that godforsaken cave."

"*Shep.*" She slid a hand into his hair. "That's horrible. Those brave men sacrificed themselves for their country." She turned his head and made him look at her.

He didn't see pity on her face, just a steady understanding.

"If the roles had been reversed, and they hadn't reached you in time, would you blame them?"

"No." His answer was instant.

She raised a brow.

Shep frowned. No, he wouldn't blame them. *Shit.* He'd always known his feelings were mixed up with losing Jenny. He had a therapist when he'd first gotten out, and she'd tried to help him untangle it, but he'd hated every second of dissecting his feelings.

Hayden's hand drifted across his shoulder. "Can I take your mind off things?" She moved against him.

He had a naked, gorgeous woman in his lap. Instantly, desire welled up, pushing out the things he'd rather not feel.

"Yeah." His voice was low.

She pushed him back on the bed and straddled him. Then she lowered her head to kiss his lips.

"Good. This time, it's going to be slow. And this time, I'm in charge."

HAYDEN WOKE to hear Shep on the phone. Morning sunlight pierced through a gap in the curtains.

She listened to the deep rumble of his voice out in the living room. She smiled, and rubbed her cheek on the sheet.

Just a few days ago, she couldn't stand him.

Now...she felt very different.

They'd slept a little during the night. She'd never thought sleeping on top of a man, held tight by his arms with her face tucked against his neck would be so comfortable.

But Shep had also woken her a few times during the night—bossy, demanding, and so hungry for her. She shivered. She had a pleasant ache between her legs, and a collection of small bruises from his teeth and fingers, and scrapes from his beard.

No, the man did not treat her like glass, and she loved that.

She trusted him, and what that hard, big body could do to hers... She shivered again. He made her feel things she'd never felt before.

He appeared in the bedroom doorway, only wearing a pair of shorts riding low on his hips. He moved very quietly for such a big man.

She noted that his face looked serious.

She sat up. "What's happened?"

"Nothing. Yet." He sat on the bed. "Vander has sent a jet. We need to sneak into the airport."

"Is it still being staked out?"

"Yes. Plus, the Iranians are lurking somewhere. None of Vander's local contacts have seen them."

A knot formed in her throat, and she swallowed. "What's our plan?"

"Miguel is dropping a car off to us. One that blends. The airport is pretty basic, and surrounded by jungle. We'll park on a side road, and trek in. Then we'll make a run for the jet."

"That sounds..."

"Dangerous." He raked a hand through his hair. "It is. But getting on that jet is the easiest and quickest way to get you out of the country."

She dragged in a breath. "Okay."

He gave her a quick kiss. "Get dressed." He strode out.

It suddenly hit her that they were leaving. She realized she was actually sad to leave this waterfront house, where it had just been the two of them for a while. A place where they could forget the rest of the world existed.

Her time with Shep was coming to a close.

Hayden bit her lip. Which was what she wanted, of course. They'd agreed to temporary and right now.

"You don't want a man, remember?" With a shake of her head, she strode to the bathroom.

Hayden quickly showered and braided her hair. She pulled on a pair of khaki pants and a white shirt.

By the time she strode into the living room, Shep was dressed. He wore a black, button-down shirt hanging open over a white T-shirt. He was sliding a handgun into the waistband of his trousers. He had his trusty, battered backpack with him, and she suspected that it was now packed with weapons.

"The car arrived," he said.

She followed him out of the house, giving it one last glance before she closed the door. There was a battered, nondescript, white car parked in the driveway.

"Here." He handed her a ball cap. As she settled it on her head, he pulled on one, as well.

"You know, I'm a little sad to leave this place." She glanced toward the pool.

Shep made a sound. "Me too."

She met his gaze, and they stared at each other for a long beat.

He jerked his head. "We need to go."

"Right."

They got in the car, and Shep started the engine. It made a weird rattling noise. He turned the wheel and maneuvered down the driveway. Soon, they were out on the road.

Hayden felt tense. She squeezed her hands together in her lap. She knew this part of their escape wasn't going to be easy. They couldn't just take a leisurely stroll into the airport like a pair of tourists.

She twisted in her seat. "Don't get hurt, okay?"

"You just focus on getting on the plane. I'm getting you out of here."

She reached across and gripped his arm. "But not at your expense. We're *both* getting out."

He just grunted.

"I mean it, Shep. By the way, is Shep short for Shepherd?"

"Yes."

"You know, I don't even know your last name. You've been inside me, and I know what sounds you make when you come, and I don't know your full name."

His gaze met hers. "Does it matter?"

"No." It really didn't. She knew *him*.

The man who'd risked his life for her. The man who

kept charging in and doing what was right. The man who hid so much under his surly exterior.

Oh, hell. She was catching feelings for him. This grumpy loner who carried the weight of the world on his shoulders.

She slumped back in her seat, her pulse thumping hard in her ears.

"What?" he asked, frowning at her.

"Nothing." She quickly turned her head to look out the window, and watched the cars driving past.

If she told him she was falling for him, he'd freak out.

For now, she'd just worry about getting safely out of the country. Then, she'd worry about finding a way to spend more time with this man.

Oh, God. She wanted to spend more time with Shep. She wanted Shep. She wanted to see his Colorado mountain. She wanted to learn his favorite foods, and what movies he liked, and what made him laugh. She also wanted to see him scowl at her. Wanted to wake up beside him.

Just focus on staying alive, Hayden.

On the drive, Shep constantly checked the mirrors. He was alert and watchful.

"Is anyone following?" she asked.

"No."

He kept to the speed limit, trying not to draw any attention. Signs for the airport appeared on the side of the road, and she knew they were getting close. Eventually, he pulled off onto a smaller road, then finally drove along a bumpy track into the trees. He stopped the car.

"Let's go," he said.

She climbed out, trying to get a handle on her nerves.

Shep circled the car, took her hand, and squeezed. His rugged face was so serious.

"You've got this, Hayden. I'll be right beside you every step of the way. You're not alone."

Hayden loved her parents. But she'd lost her mom, and her father always had other demands on his time. He'd never been fully dedicated to her. Dillon had been a liar. She'd never had someone focus just on her. Giving her what she needed and keeping her safe.

She realized that Shep did.

She yanked his head down. The kiss was fierce and furious.

When they pulled apart, he rested his forehead against hers, his chest heaving.

"I'm getting you out of here, Hayden. Plus, I'm sick of the jungle. Now move your ass." He gave her ass a smart slap.

She couldn't stop her grin.

They headed into the dense vegetation. Soon, they came up against a fence made of wire mesh. They quickly climbed over it.

Hayden wouldn't miss the jungle, either. Once again, mud was already coating her boots. They trekked on until he held up a hand. They stopped and he waved at her to crouch. She peered through the bushes.

Through the gaps in the leaves, she could see the long, gray strip of the runway. Lush greenery lay in every direction. On the far side of the runway, sat several low, white buildings trimmed with blue. They were all very basic.

Then, her gaze fell on the jet parked at one end of the runway. It was sleek and white. Her heart jumped. Several men were unloading boxes from it.

"Vander said they were going to pretend to be a flight dropping off medication." Shep pulled out a pair of binoculars, and looked around. He stiffened.

"What?" she asked.

"There are armed men by the airport buildings. They're watching the jet."

Her mouth was suddenly dry, and she licked her lips. She fought the fear down.

Seconds ticked by as they watched and waited. A bead of sweat rolled down the back of her neck.

A noisy diesel engine rumbled, and a fuel tanker pulled up beside the jet.

"Once they're done refueling, we'll run straight to the jet." Shep frowned as he scanned the runway. "We'll use the tanker to gain some cover, if we can."

She stared at the stretch of open ground between them and the jet. It was a long way to run with no cover.

"You can do this." His hand curled around the back of her neck, and he pulled her close. He pressed a hard kiss to her lips.

It steadied her. Shep was with her. They could do this.

She dragged in a deep breath. "Let's go home."

CHAPTER THIRTEEN

S hep didn't fucking like this.

There were too many guys lurking around the airport building. And probably more he couldn't see. There was too much open ground to cover to get to the jet safely. He dragged in a deep breath.

It didn't matter. He'd had worse odds before. He was getting Hayden on that plane.

He was getting her safe.

No matter what.

He watched the maintenance crew, and saw the refueling was almost finished. "Ready?"

Hayden screwed up her nose. "Ah, no, but I'll run."

"That's my girl."

Their gazes met. Shit, she wasn't his. She'd never be his.

But damned if she didn't feel like she was his.

Shep rose and tugged her up. He also pulled out his handgun. "On three."

"No, wait." Her hands clenched on his shirt. "Shep..."

He clocked the fear and nerves on her face. "I've never met a woman like you before. So damn brave. Who's been through hell, but keeps on getting back up and pushing forward."

Her face softened. "That's the nicest thing anyone's ever said to me."

"You need to meet better people," he growled.

She sucked in a breath and Shep leaned down, pressed his forehead to hers. "You've got this. I know it. You'd be a damn good recruit for Ghost Ops."

"So you *were* Ghost Ops." She pressed a hand to his cheek. "You going soft on me?"

"Nope." But he knew the word felt like a lie.

"I'm ready." She gave him a nod.

"On three. One, two, *three*."

They broke into a sprint, racing out of the trees. They ran across the grass strip toward the runway.

Shep pumped his arms, making sure Hayden was right beside him.

He angled so that the tanker was between them in the main airport buildings. He hoped to hell that no one spotted them, but he wasn't going to hold his breath.

They hit the runway, picking up speed as they sprinted toward the jet.

In the distance, shouts broke out.

Fuck.

Reports of gunfire echoed through the open air. Several men were running toward them.

Hayden's face was set, and she didn't slow down.

Then he heard the screech of tires, and his head jerked up. A black SUV was tearing out onto the tarmac.

It turned onto the runway and sped toward them.

Fucking hell. Shep stopped, and yanked Hayden behind him. He raised his weapon, took a slow breath, and focused.

He fired. Right at the driver's side windshield.

Bang. Bang. Bang.

The SUV swerved, and drove off the side of the runway into a grassy ditch.

"Come on!" He grabbed Hayden's hand.

Ahead, two men exited the jet, firing at the armed men running from the airport buildings. But several of the incoming men stopped to aim rifles their way.

Bullets hit the tarmac near Shep and Hayden. She cried out.

"Down." He yanked her down and covered her with his body. Then he raised his arm and fired. The men scattered.

The two men at the jet waved at them to hurry.

"Run, Hayden," Shep growled. "As fast as you can."

She jumped up, sprinting for the jet, a grimace on her face. He followed her, and fired several more shots at their attackers.

They were going to make it.

Shep's chest loosened, felt lighter. She'd finally be safe.

Suddenly, gunfire hit the fuel tanker.

One second, they were running, the next, the world exploded in a ball of orange flames.

He watched Hayden get lifted off her feet. She was

tossed through the air like a toy doll, and slammed into Shep. He caught her, and they both went down, rolling backward over the tarmac.

Shep hit the ground first, with Hayden on top of him. His ears were ringing, and his head was swimming. He fought through it. He'd been trained to get his bearings fast after explosions and flashbangs.

He looked up. The tanker was in pieces, flames licking the sky.

He swung his gaze over to the jet, and growled in frustration. The jet was damaged as well, peppered with shrapnel, and the tail twisted.

Fucking fuck.

Another SUV screamed onto the runway. The passengers were firing on the men running from the terminal.

Hell. New players. Probably the Iranians.

He yanked Hayden onto her feet. She was dazed and unsteady.

"*Run.*" He exploded into action, towing her behind him.

He headed for the trees.

They hit the grass and kept going. Gunfire peppered the vegetation around them.

"Oh, God." Hayden was pale, her eyes wide, but she kept running.

Shep swiveled and aimed. "Keep going." He fired.

The new SUV screeched to a halt, and the doors were flung open.

Time to go.

He turned, more gunfire echoing around them. Then,

ahead of him, Hayden jerked, and stumbled. She went down on one knee.

The world narrowed to a dark tunnel.

No. Fuck, no.

"Hayden!" he roared. He ran to her. Blood was soaking the sleeve of her white shirt.

Hayden's blood.

His stomach clenched, and it felt like it was filled with spikes.

"I am...okay." She blinked slowly, lines of pain bracketing her mouth.

He picked her up and held her tight in his arms.

Then he ran for the trees.

The greenery swallowed them, and he gritted his teeth. He didn't stop running. The team behind them would come for them. For her. They needed to get away.

They reached the car, and he opened the passenger side door and set her inside.

He quickly circled the sedan and threw himself in the driver's seat.

"Hayden. Damn." He took her arm carefully, and studied the wound. "It just grazed you." He released a shaky breath.

She nodded. "I'll be all right."

He yanked her in for a quick kiss. "We need to go." He quickly tore his outer shirt off, leaving him just wearing a T-shirt. He wadded up the fabric, and pressed it to her arm. "Hold that and keep the pressure on." He started the engine. "And get down."

She sank to the floor, curling her body up. Shep

pulled his ball cap low over his face, and pulled onto the road.

He forced himself to drive slowly, calmly, when he really wanted to speed away.

Hayden had been shot.

His gut roiled and his hands clenched on the wheel. It could have been worse. The bullet could have hit something vital. She could have died.

He tasted bile.

He couldn't fail her. He had to get her safe.

———

CROUCHED DOWN on the floor of the car, Hayden gritted her teeth and fought back the pain. She closed her eyes. It wasn't that bad, but she hated feeling the slide of blood soaking into Shep's shirt.

She swallowed. They'd barely made it out alive. She glanced up at Shep.

His jaw was tight, his face focused. His hands gripped the wheel so tight his knuckles were white.

He hadn't hesitated. He'd protected her and gotten her out.

She'd always been in awe of the Secret Service agents, the ones who risked their lives to protect the president and their family. Like those agents, Shep believed in service. He had such strong, unshakable values.

Sure, life had scratched him up and tested him, but deep down, he was a good, honorable man.

He'd hate knowing she thought he was a hero.

She rested her head against the seat. God, what now?

Suddenly, she was shaking, and she couldn't seem to stop it. She knew it was just the adrenaline crash. She tried to pull in some calming breaths. She was *not* going to lose it and make their getaway harder for Shep.

"What now?" she asked.

"We need a new plan." He didn't look at her. She knew he was pretending to be alone in the car. "How's your arm?"

"I'll live."

That muscle ticked in his jaw again.

More minutes passed. She kept waiting for someone to chase them, or for the sound of gunfire.

Shep's hands flexed on the wheel. "I'm heading into the center of Bluefields. There'll be more people there, and we can hide in plain sight."

"Sounds good."

"They'd expect us to do the opposite. I'll find somewhere where I can check your arm."

"I think the bleeding's slowing."

His hands flexed again. "I'm still checking it." He dragged in a rough breath. "Can you reach my backpack? Pull out the satellite phone and call Vander. Tell him that we need a Plan B."

She fumbled with the bag and found the satellite phone. She hit redial to place the call and pressed it to her ear.

"Lancelot?" a deep voice said.

"Um, no. This is...uh...Guinevere?"

There was a pause. "Are you okay?"

"We're both fine. But there was a gunfight. We didn't make it to the jet."

Another pause.

"Sh—I mean, Lancelot is driving us back into town. He said we need a Plan B."

"I'm on it. I'll call you back." The line went dead.

"He's on it." She tucked the phone away.

"Good." Shep turned the wheel, and then parked the car. She sat back in the seat, and saw they were on a quiet side street.

In the next second, she was dragged across the car and onto Shep's lap. He clamped her close to him, buried his face in her hair, and didn't say a word.

She pressed a palm to his chest and felt his rapid heartbeat.

"I'm all right," she reassured him.

He pulled in a ragged breath.

She pressed her lips to the side of his head. "I'm fine."

"You got shot. I didn't protect you."

Her heart squeezed. This big, strong man shouldered so much guilt, and loss, and sadness.

"You *did* protect me. In the middle of a crazy, dangerous situation." She cupped his bearded cheek. "You saved me." She reached for his hand and pulled it so that his palm pressed to her chest. "Feel my heart beating, Shep. It's doing that because of you. I'm here because of you."

She leaned forward and kissed him.

Their lips parted, tongues touched. He groaned, and instantly took control of the kiss. It was rough, passionate, with an edge. He cupped the back of her head, holding her in place for the ferocious kiss.

Soon, they were both panting. The phone ringing jerked them apart.

Shep grabbed it and pressed it to his ear. "Yeah." He paused. "Fine. That's okay. Thanks, Vander." He slid the phone away.

"We have a Plan B?" she asked.

"Yes. For now, we need to blend in, then get to the local port in just under two hours."

"We're going on a boat?" Her eyebrows winged up. "To where?"

"No idea, but I trust Vander. Someone will meet us there." Shep scowled. "But these assholes are still hunting us. We have to be careful."

She swallowed. "We can do this. Together."

He nodded. "Together."

CHAPTER FOURTEEN

They walked down a street in Bluefields. It had a beachy, low-key, Caribbean vibe, and all the buildings were painted in bright colors—blue, pink, orange, and lime green.

Shep scanned the shops and the people, holding Hayden's hand tight. He wanted her off the street. He knew the people hunting her wouldn't be far away.

Bluefields had a tiny port adjacent to the city, and a larger cargo port about eight kilometers across the bay that formed the mouth of the Escondido River.

He spotted a clothing store. Through the window, he saw an older woman at the counter, and nobody else in the store.

He pushed open the door, and towed Hayden inside. A bell tinkled.

The woman looked up. She looked to be in her sixties, with some African heritage, and long, dark hair.

"Hello, *señora.*" Like most Ghost Ops operatives,

Shep spoke several languages. "My wife is hurt. The men who hurt her are chasing us."

The woman's gaze flicked between him and Hayden. Then it settled on Hayden's injured arm and the blood soaking her shirt. Her dark-brown eyes widened.

"They're bad people," Hayden said in decent Spanish.

"*Por favor*." Shep needed to make sure that Hayden was okay. "We just need a place where I can check her wound. Where we can stay off the street." He pressed a hand to the back of Hayden's neck.

She leaned into him and shot him a tremulous smile.

The woman watched them for another beat, then nodded. "I speak English." She had a lilting accent. "I see how much you care for her. Come." She waved them toward the back of the store. A colorful curtain hung in a doorway. She pushed it aside, and beyond, lay a cramped back room. There were boxes and stock stacked against the wall, and a simple table in the center. A small sink sat in one corner.

The woman bustled around, and pulled out a small first aid kit from under the sink. "Here."

"Thank you," Shep said.

The woman nodded. "Take care of your wife."

Once she was gone, he lifted Hayden onto the table. "The shirt needs to go." He unbuttoned it.

"Wife, huh?"

He stilled, realizing the word had slipped out pretty damn easily. "We needed her help."

Hayden made a humming sound.

He pulled the shirt off, barely able to handle seeing

the blood soaking it. She had a nasty groove, and smears of blood on her skin. But thankfully, it wasn't as bad as he'd thought.

He gently touched her skin.

"Are you all right?" she asked.

"I wasn't the one who got shot."

"It's just a graze."

Then because he needed to, he cupped her cheeks and kissed her. He'd always been cool under fire, fearless. Vander had chewed him out numerous times for being too reckless.

But seeing Hayden get shot, when her body had jerked, it had wrecked him.

"I'm. All. Right." She pinched his arm and smiled. "Quit the brooding."

Then she dragged his head down and kissed him. She ended it by biting his bottom lip.

"Let me get your arm cleaned up." He opened the first aid kit and pulled out some gauze and antiseptic.

She held still as he cleaned the graze and bandaged it. Then he pressed a gentle kiss over the white bandage.

A soft look crossed her face. "What happened to the annoying super grump who only does casual and carefree? Do you kiss lots of women's boo-boos?"

"I don't fucking know where casual went." That terrified him, as well. Because somehow, Hayden Sinclair had fucking gotten under his skin. She'd found a crack and slipped right in.

He wasn't sure he liked it.

But his priority had to be getting her out of the country in one piece.

"You need some new clothes—"

There was a tinkle of the bell in the front of the shop. They both froze.

"*Señora*." It was a deep voice that held a faint accent that definitely wasn't local.

Shep pressed a finger to his lips. He headed to the curtain and pushed it aside the tiniest bit. A second later, he felt Hayden press against him, looking as well.

Shep saw a man. Dark hair, beard, brown skin. It had to be one of the Iranians.

"Are you alone?" the man asked in careful, precise Spanish.

Hayden gripped Shep's arm.

The older woman frowned. "Yes. This is my shop. What are you looking for?"

The man turned, giving Shep a better look at his face. Fuck, Shep recognized him. Ardeshir Rahim Ahmadi. A rising star in Iranian intelligence.

His Ghost Ops team had almost caught Ahmadi during a mission, but he'd managed to slip away.

Ahmadi scanned around one last time. "Nothing." Then he walked out.

The woman scowled, muttering under her breath.

Shep relaxed, then he edged through the curtain. "*Señora?*"

"You saw the rude man?" she asked.

"Yes, and we want to avoid him. We need some clothes. I can pay." Shep looked around the shop, and also spotted a dark wig resting on a mannequin. "And that."

The women burst into action.

Soon, Hayden was dressed in a long, swirling skirt of red and white, paired with a simple black T-shirt that covered the bandage on her arm. She also had a dark wig on, with her own hair tucked out of sight. It was cut in a bob style that brushed her jaw line. The older woman also handed her a pair of sunglasses.

Shep had swapped his gear for more casual clothes— brown shorts and a white shirt that stretched tight over his biceps. The woman gave him a new ball cap, and he pulled it low over his face.

He handed her some cash. "Thank you."

She took it with a nod. "Go. Take care of your love. You need each other."

Shep jerked, then cleared his throat. He didn't know anything about love, and he didn't want to. Love meant caring too much. It meant when you lost that person, it tore you apart.

He didn't bother to correct her, and he didn't look at Hayden. He just nodded and moved to the front door. He checked outside, and noted the street was clear. He took Hayden's hand, and they slipped outside.

"It's not far to the port." He tucked her hand under his arm.

She blew out a breath. "Okay." She hesitated. "You recognized that man in the store."

Shep gave a sharp nod. "He's an Iranian spy by the name of Ardeshir Ahmadi. He's dangerous."

Her fingers flexed in his. "I kind of feel like there are spotlights on me. Like everyone is going to start pointing and shouting."

"You've got this. That courage of yours will get you there."

She smiled up at him. "And you. I'm pretty damn glad you're here, Shep."

He was as well. For many reasons that he didn't have the words to describe.

THE WIG ITCHED. And nerves were like butterflies in her belly.

Almost there.

Hayden tried to act normal, and not look around, searching for the bad guys. It wasn't easy.

Shep steered her around a corner.

"How much farther?" The walk felt endless.

"We're almost there." He checked his watch. "And it's almost time to meet our contact."

When they turned onto the next street, the ocean came into view. The small port was not fancy at all. It consisted of a main concrete jetty with a few smaller ones protruding off it, and that was about it.

There were a few boats of all different sizes tied up at the jetties, bobbing up and down. One of those boats had to be waiting for them.

She picked up speed.

"Easy," Shep warned.

It was so hard to slow down. She just wanted to get out of there.

They passed some shops, and a fruit stall laden with

colorful and fragrant pineapple, passionfruit, and bananas.

Ahead of them, a man stepped out of a building.

She felt Shep's body tense.

Oh, God. Her stomach locked. The guy wore black pants and a black shirt, and had a dark complexion. But he didn't look like a local.

She swallowed. It had to be one of the men after her.

The man turned a little, and she realized it was the man from the clothing store. Ahmadi.

Shep leaned down and nuzzled her neck. "Laugh."

She managed a giggle, although it sounded a little strained. She pressed against Shep's chest. She could practically feel the man's attention on them. She prayed the wig would do its job.

Heart pounding, they walked past the man.

Thank God for Shep's steady presence. It helped her keep it together.

The boats were closer, now. They were almost there.

Suddenly, Shep shoved her away from him, and whirled. Ahmadi came at them—fast and silent. He swung an arm at Shep, but Shep blocked the hit.

Hayden gasped. She watched as the men traded blows—brutal and powerful. They were both fighting to win. Ahmadi took a step back, and pulled a knife from his belt.

No. Sunlight glinted off the blade. He slashed out. Shep leaped back. His face was blank, no emotion, just focus.

The bad guy shifted and attacked again. Shep

dodged. Then he lunged and slammed his fist into the man's head.

Ahmadi staggered and dropped the knife. Shep followed through with a blow to the man's back, then he whirled and charged.

Shep wrapped his arms around Ahmadi. Together, they slammed into the side of the building, both of them grunting. It almost looked like they were hugging, but she knew they were trying hard to get the upper hand.

Ahmadi broke free, but Shep was on him. He landed several hard hits in quick succession—stomach, sternum, throat. Hayden winced, and saw Ahmadi jerk under the blows. Then he gagged, grabbing at his neck.

With a harsh sound, he went down on one knee. Shep lifted his knee and rammed it into the man's face.

She heard the crunch of cartilage and winced again.

Ahmadi collapsed on the dirty pavement. Shep spun and grabbed her hand. "Come on."

There was no pretense now. They sprinted down the street. Her wig flew off, and her skirt billowed around her legs.

People gasped and leaped out of their way. Their shoes slapped on the cracked sidewalk.

They reached the entrance to the port, passing under a wooden archway. An old blue-and-white ferry had just pulled in, disgorging a crowd of people.

Shouts broke out behind them. She glanced over her shoulder and saw two men with guns running in their direction.

"*Move*," Shep growled.

They dodged the people.

"Where are we going exactly?" she yelled. The jetty split into two, with several small trucks nearby, unloading cargo.

Shep's brow creased. "I'm not sure."

A shot rang out. People screamed and panicked.

Ahead of her, Hayden spotted a cowering little girl. She was terrified and crying.

"Come on." Hayden grabbed the girl. "Get down." She tugged the girl down and pushed her toward some people huddled by some bags.

A man charged out of the crowd and attacked Shep.

Hayden gasped. She watched Shep whirl to meet him, and land a hard kick. But the bad guy looked intense, his mouth a grim line as he dodged. He grabbed Shep, and they grappled. Shep shifted his weight, and rammed an elbow into the man's face. The man retaliated, and thrust a punch into Shep's stomach.

No. No fucking way. He was not hurting her man.

Hayden straightened, her hands balling into fists.

And she was not a fucking victim to be hunted down like dog.

Shep and the man broke apart, and Hayden charged.

She ran right at the attacker. She hit him with her shoulder, and a shocked look crossed his face. He staggered back, and teetered on the edge of the dock.

As he fell, he grabbed for her, but strong arms yanked her back.

The bad guy landed in the murky water beside a boat with a big splash.

"Come on." Shep grabbed her hand.

Another gunman was closing in, running down the

dock. Shep fired at him, shielding her until they ran down beside a large cargo boat.

Crap, they were almost at the end of the jetty. They were trapped. There was nowhere to go, except the water.

"Here!" A local man waved at them.

Shep changed course.

"*Señor. Señorita*. Your friend sends his regards." The man waved a hand at a white speedboat bobbing on the water. The hull was stained, but it had two powerful engines on the back.

"Where do we go?" Shep asked.

"Out to sea. That's all I know. Good luck." The man saluted them.

"In," Shep ordered.

Hayden leaped into the boat, and it rocked under her. Shep followed her in, and reached for the controls. He started the engines and they rumbled to life.

More gunfire cut through the air.

Hayden ducked. Shep tossed off the rope and gunned the engine.

She almost fell on her butt as they screamed away from the dock. She gripped the side of the boat, and stared at the gunman on the dock. As they sped away, she shot him the finger.

She heard a low laugh over the engine. When she turned her head, she saw Shep looking at her. He was laughing. She smiled back at him.

CHAPTER FIFTEEN

S hep pushed for as much speed as he could from the boat's engines. The wind whipped through his hair. He glanced back at Hayden. "Stay down."

She gave a nod, her own hair whipping into her eyes.

He looked ahead, taking in the long peninsula of land that formed the barrier between the bay and the ocean. At the end of it were the main port facilities of El Bluff. There was currently a large cargo ship at the port.

He turned their boat, aiming for the gap that would lead them into the open ocean.

His gut tightened. He had no idea where they were going. The men hunting Hayden had resources, and he knew they would come after them.

"Shep!"

Even over the wind, he heard the sharp edge to her voice. He looked back over his shoulder.

And saw two speedboats racing toward them from the mainland.

Fucking hell.

She lifted her chin. "I need a gun."

Dammit. "I'll shoot." He didn't want her in the line of fire.

"I can't drive the boat. I need a weapon, Shep."

He mentally ran through a few curse words. "The backpack."

She knelt down and opened his bag. She pulled out a handgun and checked it over. He saw her swallow and knew she was afraid.

"Come here."

She maneuvered toward him, her skirt—now wet from sea spray—sticking to her legs. He yanked her in for a quick kiss.

"Don't get hurt," he growled. "If you get shot again..."

He couldn't handle it. If she got hurt, he would burn the world down.

She cupped his cheek. "Get us wherever the hell we're going, and I'll keep the goon squad off us."

Over the next few minutes, the speedboats gained on them. They were sleek and newer than their boat, with more power.

A gunshot whizzed past and Shep tensed. Not close. Just a warning shot.

"Cut your engines," a voice said over a loudspeaker. "Give us the woman."

Shep gave them the finger.

The boats continued to get closer. Hayden crouched down at the side of their boat, then popped up, and aimed. She fired.

A second later, the bad guys returned gunfire. Shep

ducked down by the controls, checking that Hayden was down as well. Bullets hit the side of their boat.

He heard Hayden cursing.

"Hayden?" he roared.

"I'm *fine*." She popped up and fired again.

The two boats chasing them split up. Hayden swiveled, aiming at the one that was getting closer.

"Hold on." He threw their boat into a turn. They cut across the waves, roaring past El Bluff and into open waters. The waves got heavier and larger.

Hayden kept firing.

One boat veered sharply, hit a wave, and went airborne. It tipped over, men falling into the ocean.

"Hell, yeah!" She grinned at him as she reloaded.

For a second, Shep felt like he got tunnel vision. All he could see was her smile. All he could see was Hayden.

He felt a burn in his chest. *What did that mean?* He had a suspicion, but he didn't like it.

The other boat raced closer, and he shook his head to focus. Hayden fired, but several men on the approaching speedboat returned fire.

"Get down!" Shep yelled.

She dropped to the floor.

A bullet hit the boat close to Shep. *Hell.* His jaw was tight as he threw them into more evasive maneuvers.

But it wouldn't be enough. These assholes were gaining on them, and he was outnumbered.

They'd kill him and take Hayden.

He ground his teeth together and pulled his own weapon from his waistband. Controlling the boat with one hand, he fired with the other.

The speedboat pulled in behind them. There was a barrage of bullets, and he heard Hayden cry out.

"I'm okay." She scurried toward him.

Their engines spluttered. *No.* Their attackers had been targeting their engines.

A second later, the engines died.

Their boat slowed, bobbing up and down on the waves.

"Shep." Her worried gaze met his.

They were sitting ducks. His chest felt like it was filled with rocks. He pulled her to his chest and watched the other boat coming closer.

Ahmadi stood at the front of it. He was glaring at them. Shep took in the man's bloody nose and swelling face, and felt a punch of satisfaction.

"Whatever happens, stay strong," Shep murmured.

Her hands clenched in his shirt.

He gripped her chin and tipped it up. "They'll kill me and take you."

She made a terrified sound.

"You have to stay strong. You have to stay alive."

"*No.*" Pure panic flared in her dark eyes. "I'm not letting them hurt you."

God, she was something.

It would break something inside him to watch them take her.

Then Shep heard another sound. He frowned. He saw some of the bad guys frowning as well, then start pointing into the distance.

Shep turned his head. Hayden gasped.

Two sleek, black zodiac boats were speeding toward

them. Both were filled with several men. A few of them were armed.

The man in the lead boat had a tall, lean, muscled form.

Shep smiled. "Change of plans. The cavalry's arrived."

One zodiac sped past them, and gunfire filled the air. The second circled around behind Ahmadi's boat and opened fire.

Several bad guys' bodies shuddered under the impact, while some managed to dive overboard.

The man in the lead zodiac held the rifle with ease, and had the balance of a man used to the ocean.

"Who's that?" Hayden asked.

"An old friend. Lorenzo 'Ren' Santoro."

"A Ghost Ops buddy."

"I can neither confirm nor deny."

She shook her head and smiled.

They watched as Ren lifted his rifle and aimed at the bad guy's boat. His shot hit the fuel tank.

The boat exploded.

Shep swiveled to cover Hayden.

———

HAYDEN WILLED her racing heart to slow down. Her body couldn't quite comprehend that she and Shep were all right.

They were safe.

For a moment, it had seemed that everything was lost.

She'd been terrified that she'd have to watch Shep be killed.

Now...

She clung to him as one of the zodiacs pulled up alongside their disabled boat.

"Shep, fancy meeting you here."

Ren stood with his feet apart, a rifle in his hand. He smiled.

Hayden blinked. He was handsome in that way that dazed you a little. He had a long, chiseled face, tanned skin, and deep, brown eyes. His smile was wide, with a sinful edge.

"Ren, you're a fucking sight for sore eyes," Shep said.

"I knew you missed me, even if I never missed your surly, brooding ass."

"He does know you," Hayden said.

Shep squeezed her hip. "Permission to come aboard."

Ren inclined his head. "Permission granted."

Shep helped Hayden over. Ren took her hand, and guided her into the zodiac, shooting her a wide, sexy smile.

"Ms. Sinclair, it's a pleasure." He was talking like they were meeting at a party—not in the middle of a shootout on the ocean. "I'm Lorenzo, but please call me Ren."

"Thanks for the rescue."

"Believe me, I'm well practiced at saving Shep's ass."

Shep, with his backpack over his shoulder, stepped aboard. The two men smiled at each other, then hugged, slapping each other's backs.

"How the hell did you end up here?" Shep asked. "I

thought you were somewhere in the middle of the Pacific."

Ren smiled. "Vander. I'll share all the details once we're back on my ship." He waved a hand at the seats.

They sat, and the zodiac's engines fired up. The boat sped off, rising and falling on the waves as they powered farther out to sea.

That's when Hayden noticed the white ship in the distance. It looked large and fancy, with lots of antennas on top and a crane built into the back.

Shep slung an arm around her shoulders, and she leaned into him.

They were safe. She couldn't quite believe it. Elation pushed up through the fear, shock, and adrenaline.

They pulled up at the back of the ship. There was a lower deck with several people waiting for them. They were helped aboard.

Ren handed his rifle off to someone, calling out orders to a few people. She saw several of the people looking at her with interest, and realized that they knew who she was.

Turning, she took in the large crane and several underwater submersibles stored on the ship's deck. They looked like something out of a science fiction movie.

Ren turned, smiled, and slapped Shep's shoulder. "It's damn good to see you. Welcome aboard the *Atalanta*. The finest research vessel on the sea."

"You always loved the water."

"Once a SEAL, always a SEAL." Then Ren's handsome face turned serious. "We were conducting marine research off the coast of Panama. Vander called a few days ago."

Shep raised a brow. "A few days ago?"

Ren nodded. "I was Plan B. We headed this way in case you needed us."

Shep shook his head. "Vander always has a contingency plan."

"Or ten." Ren's dark gaze moved to Hayden. "Ms. Sinclair—"

"It's Hayden, please. Anyone who saves my life gets to use my first name."

He gave her a mesmerizing smile.

An older man with a weathered face and a long, black beard speckled with gray appeared. He wore a polo shirt with the ship's logo on it—a circle with a crashing wave inside.

"Everyone all right?" the man asked.

"They're fine," Ren said. "Shep, Hayden, this is Captain Shroff."

The captain nodded. "I'm glad you're both okay. Whatever you need, Ren will see to it."

"Thank you," Shep said.

"It's our pleasure to help." The captain's light-blue gaze fell on Hayden. "Ms. Sinclair, we've been informed that your father is sending a helicopter from a nearby Navy ship tomorrow morning."

Hayden felt a clutch in her chest. She was leaving? Tomorrow. In less than half a day, she'd be gone, whisked away.

Away from Shep.

"Right. Thanks."

Shep was still and silent beside her.

"You've been through a rough time," Ren continued. "I'm sure you'd like to shower, put on some clean clothes. I have cabins arranged for you."

"I need to stay close to her," Shep said, voice tight.

Ren lifted a brow, speculation on his face, but he nodded. "Of course. After you've freshened up, why don't we meet for an early dinner in the mess? I bet you need a drink."

CHAPTER SIXTEEN

S hep followed Hayden and one of the ship's crew down to their quarters. It wasn't quite as tight as he'd imagined.

"Sorry we don't have any of the upper staterooms available." The young man, Toby, headed down some stairs. "But the main crew cabins aren't too bad."

"We're only here one night," Hayden said. "And I've spent time in tents on hot, steamy digs, so I'm not fussy."

Toby looked back and smiled at her. "You aren't what I imagined the president's daughter would be like."

"I get that a lot."

Toby's smile widened.

Shep fought the urge to hit him, but settled for a scowl.

"Here you go." Toby waved at one of the many doors along the corridor. "This cabin here, and the one next door—"

"Thanks," Shep growled.

The young man glanced at him and swallowed. "Right. If you need anything, I'll just be down..."

"We've got it," Shep said.

With a nod, the man headed off down the corridor.

Hayden cocked a brow. "You scared the poor guy."

Shep grunted and led her inside the first cabin.

It had a single bed—but at least it was extra wide—that sat under the window. There was a built-in desk and cupboard, and a tiny adjoining bathroom.

Energy was still pumping through his system. They'd barely gotten away today. So many things could've gone wrong.

Hell, one thing had gone wrong—Hayden had been shot.

He heaved in a breath, and fought for some control. "How's your arm?"

"It's fine, Shep." She turned to face him and smiled. "We made it. We're safe."

He growled. "I won't consider you safe until you're back on US soil."

Her face changed, shutting down. "Which will be soon. The helicopter's coming tomorrow."

They stared at each other, tension filling the space between them.

Tomorrow, she'd be gone.

Shep would go back to where he belonged. Alone.

Something snapped inside him. He surged forward and hauled her into his arms.

She gasped. "*Shep*."

He pressed her back to the wall, and buried his face

in her neck. He breathed in her scent, mixed with the smell of the sea.

"You're so tense." Her hands kneaded his shoulders. "We're both safe now. You can relax. I'm safe thanks to you."

"I..." He shuddered. "I can't get a grip on... I just need to know you're safe. Know you're okay."

She nuzzled the side of his head. "Take what you need, Shep. What we both need." She bit his ear lobe.

He moved his head and kissed her. He speared his tongue into her mouth, wanting to plunder. He wanted her to feel nothing but him. She bit his bottom lip, pressing her body into him. They surged against each other—hungry, needy, fierce.

Shep eased back enough that he could shove her damp skirt up. He reached underneath and ripped her underwear off.

"*Yes*," she said breathlessly. "Hurry."

He freed his cock, and ran the swollen head through her slick folds. She gasped and gripped his shoulders hard, then the next second, he surged inside her.

She cried out.

"Who's inside you, Hayden?"

"*You*," she moaned. "Shep."

"*Mine*." He pumped inside her. Damn, she was tight. "Yes."

He kept thrusting. He knew he was being too rough, but he couldn't stop. He needed to stamp himself on her, memorize everything about her.

She clung to him, whispering hotly in his ear. Urging him on. "I'm so close. Shep, *please*."

On his next thrust, she came. She cried out his name, and her pussy clamped down on his cock. The sensations threw him into his own climax.

He groaned, long and loud, as he emptied himself inside her. She arched in his arms as her own pleasure took her.

Afterward, they were both wrecked. Shep stayed where he was, pinning her to the wall. He was half afraid if he moved, he'd collapse.

"I was rough."

"I noticed." She moved her hand across his shoulders. "It was awesome."

Her touch, and the clear satisfaction in her voice, soothed him. "Let's shower." He pushed back and let her legs fall to the floor. "Then I'll check your arm."

"Mmm." She gave him a lazy, pleased smile.

They took a shower in the tiny stall, and he washed her hair. Afterward, he checked and rebandaged her arm.

Both of them dressed in the ship uniforms they found in the closet. Shep wasn't really a polo shirt kind of guy, but it would do. The navy-blue shirt had the ship's logo on it.

"I need to finish drying my hair." She ran her fingers through the damp strands. "Go, catch up with your friend. I'll be there soon."

He hesitated. A part of him didn't want to let her out of his sight.

"I'm safe here." She stepped up to him and pressed a kiss to his bearded jaw.

Reluctantly, he left her in the cabin and headed up to the mess. The spacious dining room had a wall of

161

windows framing the water, and was filled with wooden tables that were bolted to the floor. He heard the sounds of cooking from the adjoining galley. He also spotted Ren behind a small bar, mixing a drink.

"Shep." Ren smiled. "I just made a cocktail for Hayden. I figured you'd want a beer." He reached down to a small fridge, then set two green bottles on the bar. Shep took one of the bottles of Heineken.

"Nice ship. Well-equipped and spacious for a research vessel."

"The *Atalanta* is owned and funded by a billionaire dedicated to ocean research. He doesn't spare any expense."

"Nice gig."

Ren nodded. "It is. And Captain Shroff and I get on well."

"So, you're the second in command?"

"Yep." Ren leaned on the bar. "The XO. A combination of second officer and head of security. Suits me." Ren's gaze ran over Shep, then his friend grinned. "You look...like a man who just spent some quality time with his woman."

Shep growled and took a sip of his beer.

"No judgment. She's lovely. And smart, despite the fact that she's tangling with you which is somewhat questionable."

Ren had always been the one to tease and poke at everyone on the team. Shep was used to it. "It's just temporary." Suddenly, he found it hard to swallow his beer.

"Really?"

"Yeah."

Ren shook his head. "You're an idiot, Shep."

Shep set the bottle down on the bar with a crack. "Don't go there."

"You're protective of her, and if you think I haven't noticed that you watch her like she's the best thing you've ever seen in your life, you're wrong." Ren paused. "And she looks back."

"She's the daughter of the *president*. She's a career archeologist. She's beautiful, smart—"

"It doesn't matter whose daughter she is if you care. And you deserve smart and beautiful."

Shep looked away.

"If you love her..."

"Love?" Shep's throat went tight. "Fuck, Ren. I don't know anything about love."

"You do. You loved your sister. You loved the team."

"Fat lot of good it did Jenny, or Miles, Charlie, and Julio."

Ren's mouth tightened. "We all miss them, but we honor them. We remember the good times. They knew you loved them like brothers. And I bet Jenny did too."

"*Fuck*." Shep snatched up the beer again and tossed some back.

"It's time to accept you're human, Shep. Like the rest of us. You were just a kid when your sister died. It was the adults in your life that failed her, not you. And Charlie, Miles, and Julio knew what they signed up for. They died heroes, so don't tarnish that legacy with guilt. If you don't hold onto that woman, they'd kick your ass."

"You already want to kick his ass?" Hayden appeared

in the doorway of the mess. "I think he makes everyone feel that way. It's his superpower."

Shep tensed, wondering how much she'd heard. But she moved over to him and touched his arm, and the tension inside him eased.

"Hayden, I have a cocktail just for you." Ren nabbed the glass on the bar and held it out. "I call it the Deep Ocean Blue."

"Why thank you." She sipped the blue drink and made an appreciative sound. "Although I wouldn't have said no to a beer."

Ren glanced at Shep. "You lucky bastard. Now, let's eat. Our chef's cooked up some fresh mahi-mahi."

They sat at one of the tables by the window, and shared a meal. Ren was charming to Hayden, flirting with her just to annoy Shep. He'd always had a way with the ladies. Whenever they'd been on R&R, women had flocked around Ren.

Although, only one woman had ever gotten under Ren's skin. One woman he avoided. It was maybe why Ren was out here on a ship in the middle of the ocean.

"How's Bradshaw?" Shep asked.

Ren smiled at the mention of his best friend and mentor. "It's Captain Bradshaw now. And he's at Coronado, putting potential SEAL recruits through their paces."

Tom Bradshaw had been Ren's commanding officer when he'd been a Navy SEAL, before he'd joined Ghost Ops. The men had become best friends, despite Tom being a little older.

Shep sipped his beer. "And Halle?"

Ren's smile slipped a fraction. "Great, I hear. She's at college studying marine biology."

Tom had married young, and had a beautiful daughter.

One that Ren had always been protective about.

Ren leaned back in his chair. "Now, let me tell you about the time Shep got himself in a whole lot of trouble in a back alley in Marrakech."

Hayden leaned forward, putting her elbows on the table. "Really?"

Shep groaned. "He's a liar, Hayden."

"He almost got himself engaged to the daughter of a local merchant. There was a miscommunication."

Hayden laughed and Shep rolled his eyes. Ren was the king of embellishing a good story.

Ren regaled them with several stories. Shep liked hearing Hayden's laugh. A few times, she had to wipe tears out of her eyes.

"Well, I need to do rounds of the ship." Ren stood. "It's been a pleasure, Hayden." He reached for her hand.

"Kiss her and I'll have to punch you," Shep warned.

Ren looked amused. "After the last few days, I'm sure you two would like to get some sleep." Ren winked. "Or not."

Hayden's cheeks turned pink, and Shep shot his friend the finger. With a wave, Ren strode out, calling goodbyes to a few other crew members at other tables.

"I like your friend," Hayden said.

"He's annoying."

She reached across the table and took his hand. "You love him like a brother. It's clear."

Shep lifted a shoulder. "I tolerate him."

She stroked her finger down his palm. "And me? Do you tolerate me?"

"You've grown on me."

"Good." She cocked her head. "How about we test out that bunk in the cabin? I've never had sex on a ship."

"I fucked you as soon as we came aboard."

"Okay, I've never had sex on a ship while *lying* down."

Shep couldn't help but smile. "I guess we'd better rectify that."

Losing himself in Hayden's body was a lot better than thinking about what the morning would bring.

The moment when he'd watch her walk away.

***

HAYDEN WOKE to darkness and Shep's hot, hard body wrapped around her from behind. This bed was definitely not designed for two, or a man Shep's size, but they'd managed.

It took a second to remember where they were. The *Atalanta*.

After dinner, they'd had slow sexy times. He'd been silent the entire time, purely focused on her. He'd made her come over and over again, like a man on a mission.

Like he was memorizing her.

Her belly coiled into a tight knot. Neither of them had talked about the fact that she was leaving tomorrow.

It was then she realized that Shep was awake, his body tense.

"Shep?"

"Shh."

Her shoulders tightened. His tone made her throat close. "What's wrong?"

"The engines have stopped."

Oh, God, he was right. The ship was silent and not moving. They were just rocking on the waves. "Maybe there's engine trouble?"

"Maybe." He rose. "I'll check it out."

She watched his shadowed form as he pulled on his clothes, then tucked a handgun into the waistband of his cargo pants.

She sat up. "You don't think it's engine trouble."

"No."

She got up as well, and scrambled around to find her clothes.

"Hayden, I need you somewhere safe."

"Okay. I'll lock the door."

He shook his head. "Not here. Somewhere no one knows. If someone is on the ship, and they question the crew, they'll find out that you're in this cabin."

And just like that, fear roared back in. She'd thought she was safe, and now that security had been ripped away. Tears threatened, and she pinched her nose, and pushed the panic back down. "Tell me where to hide."

His big hand cupped her face. "Good girl." He took her hand in his.

Silently, they left the cabin and hurried down the narrow hall. He led her through a door, then down another hall. It felt like a maze. They entered a small room, and she saw a low light on over a sink. It illuminated several washing machines and dryers. Shep opened a closet door. It was mostly filled with stacks of folded linen.

He rearranged some, making a space for her. "In here."

"Great," she muttered. Then she spun and gripped his shirt. "Listen, do *not* get hurt. That's an order."

He gave her a hard kiss, then urged her into the bottom of the closet. "Stay out of sight until either Ren or I come back to get you."

He closed the door and was gone.

Hayden sat curled up in the darkness, straining to hear anything. The only thing she could hear was her rapid heartbeat. She sighed, resting her chin on her knees.

She realized Shep hadn't responded to her order to stay safe.

She closed her eyes. "Be safe, Shep, or you'll answer to me."

HE NEEDED TO FIND REN.

Shep slipped down the corridor, listening for anything. All the cabins were quiet, and he hoped to hell the ship's crew stayed asleep.

He went up the stairs and onto the deck. A cool wind blew off the sea, and tugged at his hair and shirt.

Moving quickly, he navigated the deck, sticking to the shadows. The ship had a large crane at the back, and several large submersibles locked onto the deck.

He tried to see any movement, but everything was still.

Too still.

He circled around some stacked gear, and that's when he saw a dark smear on the deck. *Shit*. He crouched and touched it. Blood.

Rising, he continued on. That's when he saw a body lying on the deck.

Dammit. It was one of the *Atalanta* crew. He bent over and touched the man's neck. Alive, but he'd clearly been hit on the head.

Shep pulled his gun and rose. He needed to get to Ren's stateroom on the other side of the ship. He hadn't gone far when he noted puddles of water on the deck.

Someone had come aboard.

He hurried down the deck, and didn't go far when he heard voices ahead, talking in hushed whispers. His jaw tightened and he crouched down behind a submersible. No one was getting Hayden. He darted across to another submersible, moving fast.

He paused in the shadows, straining to hear what the men were saying.

Then he sensed someone behind him. He tensed and raised his gun. On the next breath, he spun around—

And came face to face with Ren's Glock.

"Dammit, Shep," Ren muttered.

"We have visitors," Shep murmured.

"Yeah, I realized when the engines stopped. How many?"

"There are two ahead talking. One of your men is down at the back of the ship, but he was breathing."

"Whoever they are, they'll pay." Ren's tone was lethal.

"How many security guys have you got?" Shep had noted that only Ren and two other men had been armed in the zodiacs.

"Two. Diaz and Corbin. Corbin was on night watch, so he's probably the one who's injured. I sent Diaz down to assist the maintenance guys to get the engines back up and running."

"Just us then."

Ren made a sound. "More than enough. Ready to do our thing?"

Shep nodded. "I've got your back."

"And I've got yours. And your girl's, too."

Shep didn't bother arguing that she wasn't his, because fuck it, Hayden Sinclair felt like his. "They'll head for Hayden's cabin."

"You stashed her somewhere?"

Shep nodded.

"Then let's intercept our uninvited guests."

They moved together. Ren had always been good at stalking in the darkness. He could get right up close to the enemy without them ever knowing he was there. He moved like a predator.

They fell into motion like they'd never stopped working together.

Shep realized that the two men who'd been talking had headed down to the cabins. He hurried forward and checked the stairs, then nodded at Ren. They moved downward.

Keeping his gun up, Shep moved into the corridor.

It was quiet.

He took a few more steps, then saw a shadow move into the hall, coming out of his and Hayden's cabin.

"It's empty," the man whispered. "She must be here somewhere close."

"Ahmadi's hacked the ship's CCTV. He'll find her."

Rage filled Shep. They were *not* getting Hayden. They needed taking down, once and for all.

Shep charged. He came in silent, and rammed into the man.

The guy grunted and dropped his gun.

Shep snapped an elbow up, then landed a flurry of punches into the man's body—brutal and unrelenting. "You're never going to touch her, asshole."

A second intruder rushed out of the cabin, a knife in hand. He aimed right at Shep.

Ren lunged in, and kicked the knife out of the man's hand. Then he gripped the back of the man's neck, and slammed his head into the wall.

The man made a choked sound and collapsed. Shep landed the side of his palm hard into his attacker's throat. The man gagged. Shep's next punch knocked him out.

"Tie them up." Ren handed him a zip tie.

Together, they dragged the pair into an empty cabin and restrained them.

"One's got an earpiece." Shep pulled it out and slipped it into his ear.

"I've narrowed down the target's location. Laundry room. Closing in."

Shep's blood ran ice cold. Ahmadi's voice. No. *No.*

For a second, Jenny's lifeless body flashed before his eyes. Then Julio, Miles, and Charlie in body bags.

You failed them. You're always too late. You're useless.

It was his grandfather's voice.

"Shep?"

He jerked, saw Ren watching him.

Fuck it. He wouldn't be too late this time. He *had* to get to Hayden.

"There's another one after Hayden." Shep charged down the corridor.

I'm coming, princess.

CHAPTER SEVENTEEN

All she could hear was her raspy breathing and the thud of her heart.

Hayden twisted her hands together. *Please let Shep be okay.*

This nightmare just wouldn't end. These people after her just wouldn't stop.

She rested her head against the side of the closet. She'd wanted to ask Shep if they could see each other after they got back to the States. She pressed a palm to her stomach. But she'd chickened out. She'd let him kiss her, touch her, and she'd gotten lost in pleasuring each other.

If he said no...

Her stomach did a sickening turn. She suspected that it would hurt worse than when she'd caught Dillon doing his assistant on his desk.

After all this is over, she'd woman up and talk to Shep.

She wanted time with him.

She just wanted him—grumpy, antisocial tendencies and all.

That's when she heard a noise.

Hayden held her breath, straining to hear. Her pulse leaped. *Was Shep back? Was it over?*

The sound of slow footsteps. Cautious. Then she heard doors opening and closing.

Her chest and stomach clenched. Someone was searching the room, and it wasn't Shep.

Shit, what should she do? Whoever it was, they were getting closer.

Anger burst inside her. It was one of *them.* She wasn't going to just sit and wait for the asshole to find her.

She'd go on the offensive.

Okay, so she didn't have a weapon, but she had a lot to fight for.

A stubborn grump of a man she wanted to spend more time with.

Steeling herself, Hayden burst out of the closet and rammed straight into a man.

He grunted. She rammed her shoulder into him again. He hit a washing machine with a dull clang.

"Finally," he said. "There you are."

That voice. Her gaze whipped to his face, and she took in the swelling and bruising.

"Ahmadi."

He smiled. "Ah, you know who I am."

The anger inside her exploded. This man was someone who could kidnap and kill with no compunction.

He wasn't the one who'd killed Maria, but because of

men like him, she was dead. Hayden gritted her teeth, pulled her arm back and punched him in the stomach.

Growling, he grabbed her. They spun in a circle, which was hard in the tight confines of the laundry.

He shoved her hard against the wall and pain rocketed through her. She rammed a hit toward his injured face, but his arm snapped out and he gripped her wrist.

His hand squeezed like a vise, grinding the delicate bones of her wrist together. She grimaced. Then he sank his other hand into her hair.

"You're coming with me," he said, tone hard. "Do it quietly, or I'll kill anyone you wake up."

Her stomach dropped. Shep would come. She just had to stall this guy.

"This isn't going to end the way you want," she said.

Ahmadi tugged on her hair, and she cried out.

"Yes, it will. I *always* complete my mission."

"Fuck you!" She yanked her wrist free of his hold, then rammed her fingers into his eyes.

He yelled and shoved her.

Hayden fell back on the floor, then scrambled backward.

Ahmadi dropped his hand from his face. He glared at her and advanced. "You've been a lot more trouble than I anticipated, but I have my orders."

Her heart beat hard and fast in her chest. *Think, Hayden. You need to stop him.*

"Oh, she's trouble all right. *My* trouble."

Shep stepped into the laundry room.

Relief washed over her. But as the two men faced off, fear was like a shot to her bloodstream.

Before she could take a breath, they charged at each other.

Shep and Ahmadi slammed into each other. They traded several fast hits, and she saw Shep's weapon hit the floor.

The men clashed, and for a second, it looked like they were embracing, barely moving.

But she knew they both were straining against the other, trying to land vicious blows. She heard them grunt. They spun, ramming into the wall, they spun again and rammed into the opposite wall.

Ahmadi managed to pin Shep to the wall and hammered punches into his torso.

No. Hayden leaped up. She swung her arm and rammed a fist into Ahmadi's lower back.

He let out a roar, and loosened his hold on Shep. He whirled to face her.

She saw death on his face.

SHIT. The fucker hadn't broken any of Shep's ribs, but he'd definitely come close. A sharp pain cut through his side like a piercing scream.

But as he saw the man focus on Hayden, Shep's pain receded.

Not happening. He couldn't lose Hayden. Whatever it took, he was keeping her safe.

Shep kicked Ahmadi, then hammered another kick to the man's knee.

With a vicious curse, Ahmadi staggered. Shep

opened a dryer door and slammed it into the asshole's face.

Ahmadi let out a strangled cry. Yeah, Shep knew the blow to his already-broken nose would be agony.

When the man fell on the floor, breathing heavily, Shep advanced.

Time to end this.

Hayden suddenly froze, looking behind Shep. "Look out!"

A heavy blow hit the back of his head.

Black spots danced in front of his eyes and pain rocketed down his spine.

He collapsed to his knees. Dizziness made the world swirl, his vision blurred. Another blow hit his head and he heard Hayden scream.

He couldn't control his body and he fell forward, flat onto the floor.

"I'll take care of him," an accented voice said.

"No time." Ahmadi pushed to his feet and grabbed Hayden. "We need to get to the speedboat and get out of here. We can't risk alerting anyone else on the ship."

No. Fuck. Shep fought through his muddy head. He couldn't let them take her. He tried to push through the pain-soaked fog.

He had to save Hayden. He couldn't be too late. Not again.

"Let me go!"

Even though he couldn't move, he saw Hayden struggling. Ahmadi lifted her off her feet and carried her out.

No. Shep felt like his insides had been ripped in two. He closed his eyes, nausea swamping him.

Keep going, Shep. It was Jenny's sweet voice in his head.

Get up, soldier. Miles' no-nonsense voice.

Quit laying around, Barlow. Charlie's familiar teasing tone.

You've got this. Julio's encouragement.

Shep pushed up onto his hands and knees. Everything swam.

He *had* to get to Hayden.

Just the thought of her steadied him. He held onto that thought, used it to power him. He gripped the edge of the nearby bench and hauled himself to his feet.

He staggered out of the laundry, hoping to hell he wasn't going to puke. As he passed his cabin, he stopped and found his backpack. Dragging in a breath, he pulled out another handgun.

Then he was back out in the corridor, his focus on reaching his woman. He climbed up the stairs, every step hurting, but he kept going.

At the top, he heard a sound and whipped his gun up.

And saw Ren.

"Where the hell have you been?" Shep growled.

"Got waylaid by two others. Hayden?"

"They took her," Shep growled.

"*Fuck.*"

"Come on."

"How badly are you hurt?" Ren frowned at him. "You're unsteady."

"Took a blow to the head. I'm fine." Nothing was keeping him from Hayden.

Ren blew out a breath. "Lucky you have a hard head."

Together, they jogged down the deck. Shep noticed Ren was limping, and guessed his fight hadn't been easy either.

Then Shep spotted movement in the darkness ahead. He slowed, and saw the two large silhouettes, and a smaller one struggling against them.

Shep wanted to run in, but he gritted his teeth and made himself think.

Suddenly, Hayden ripped herself free.

"Go," Shep said to Ren.

His friend burst into action, firing his weapon.

Ahmadi and his friend scattered, and Hayden ducked and ran.

Shep headed her way.

So did Ahmadi.

No, you don't.

Shep circled around a submersible. He saw Hayden with her back to him, and grabbed her arm.

She screamed.

"Hey, it's me."

"Shep!" She whirled. "Oh, thank God."

He raised his weapon. He didn't see Ahmadi. *Where the hell was he?*

"Come on." Shep tugged her away. "Let's—"

A figure leaped off the top of the submersible. It hit Shep, driving him to the deck. Hayden yelled.

Shep's gun flew out of his hand, and shocking pain reverberated through his torso. Fighting it, he surged up, wrestling his attacker.

An elbow to his face knocked him back. Then the fucker hammered a fist into Shep's hurting ribs.

The world wavered and he groaned.

Ahmadi rose, a gun in his hand. He aimed it at Shep.

"No!" Hayden leaped onto the man's back.

Ahmadi cursed in Farsi and spun, trying to knock her off.

Gunfire pinged off the submersible. Cursing, Shep turned and crawled into cover. He saw another Iranian advancing.

Ahmadi flung Hayden off, and she hit the deck and rolled.

Shep grabbed her ankle and dragged her toward him. As more gunfire hit around them, he covered her body with his.

"Stay down," he ordered.

More bullets pinged around them.

"Shep—"

He saw his gun nearby on the deck and he reached out for it.

Ahmadi stepped into view, weapon aimed at Shep.

Shep's fingers closed around the hilt of his weapon. He whipped the gun up.

They both fired.

In slow motion, he watched as Ahmadi fell backward.

But Shep felt pain tear through his chest.

This time, he couldn't push back the agony. Blackness swamped him and dragged him down.

HAYDEN STARED at Ahmadi lying just two feet away from her. She sucked in a sharp breath. Blood pooled beneath him, and his lifeless eyes were open.

He was dead.

She only felt relief. Then she heard running feet coming in their direction.

"Restrain any intruders," she heard Ren order.

Thank God.

"It's over, Shep." He was still a heavy weight on top of her. "You can get up now, Rambo. I'm safe."

He didn't move. She tried to shift and realized he was a dead weight.

"Shep?" Sharp panic rose inside her. "*Shep.*"

She pushed at him, and felt something wet soaking into her shirt.

No. Oh, no. "Ren!" Her voice was shrill. "Shep's hurt."

She heard Ren curse.

Shep's weight was lifted off her. Hayden spun to her knees, panic like a trapped bird in her chest.

Ren laid Shep flat on his back, tearing his shirt open.

Blood.

So much blood.

"*Shep.*" She scrambled closer.

"Wilson, bring your kit," Ren barked toward the crewmember nearby. Then he looked at Hayden, his handsome face serious. "He's been shot."

A trim, older man appeared. He had a neat, gray goatee and a shaved head. He knelt down and opened a large, black backpack. Then he leaned over Shep and got to work.

Ren sat back, a muscle in his jaw ticking. "Diaz, get the dead bodies bagged and dealt with."

She barely heard as Ren issued more orders to his crew.

The medic made a frustrated sound. "Gunshot wound to the upper chest. He's losing blood fast."

Ren pulled Hayden back a little. "Wilson's an excellent medic. Let him do his job."

"Shep was protecting me. He got shot protecting me." Fear and pain felt like they were wrapping around her organs, squeezing tight. "He's protected me since the moment I first met him." A small, hiccupping laugh escaped her. "I punched him that first time."

Ren gripped her arm. "He makes a lot of people feel like doing that."

She kept her gaze locked on Shep's still face. He was so pale. So not like him. There was no scowl, no glare.

"I can't lose him," she whispered. "He's damn well made me start falling for him."

"He's going to be *fine*." Ren smoothed a hand down her arm. "As soon as I knew we had intruders aboard, I had the captain call for help. A helicopter is incoming from the USS *Blackburn*. They have a full medical team on the ship. He's going to be fine."

Ren sounded like he was trying to convince himself as much as her.

She crouched down and touched Shep's hair. He turned his head toward her.

Her pulse leaped. "Shep? I'm here."

For a second, his eyes open. They were unfocused. "Hay-den."

182

"Yes. I'm here."

"Safe?"

"Yes. You saved me. You're going to be all right."

He blinked slowly, then groaned. His eyes closed again.

"Hold on, Shep."

"I've slowed the bleeding," Wilson said, tone grim, "but it's not stopping. He needs surgery."

Nausea hit her. She leaned over Shep. "Hold on, you hear me. If you don't, I'll be so pissed."

"Hayden, why don't you go and get cleaned up?" Ren suggested.

There was blood all over her. Shep's blood. She stared at her hands. "No. I'm staying with him."

After that everything became a whirl. She kept her focus on Shep, like she could will him to stay alive. Eventually, she heard the *thump, thump, thump* of rotor blades and soon a helicopter swung in over to the ship, lights bright in the night sky.

"The helicopter is here," she whispered to Shep. "We're getting you to a Navy ship." Her voice broke. "I'm *really* mad you got shot."

Men in Navy uniforms appeared, carrying a stretcher.

"Ma'am, you need to move back," one of the men said.

She hesitated, but Ren tugged her backward. "Come on, Hayden."

Before she knew it, she was sitting in a large helicopter with a headset on. In front of her, the medical team worked on Shep.

They lifted off, flying out over the dark ocean. The *Atalanta's* lights got smaller and smaller.

Shep didn't regain consciousness. He was so damn still.

God. She twisted her hands together in her lap.

"He's strong and stubborn." Ren's steady voice came through the headset. He was sitting beside her.

She nodded, tears threatening. Shep was both those things. He was the strongest man she knew.

She wasn't sure how long the helicopter journey was, but when she saw a large ship ahead, relief punched through her. As they came into land, there was a hive of activity on the deck below.

"He's ready for transport to sick bay," someone said.

"Let's get ready to move as soon as we touch down," a man responded.

Hayden ripped her headset off. She reached out and touched Shep's cheek. His skin was cool. She leaned close and pressed a kiss to his temple. "You get better fast because I've changed my mind. Casual is *not* happening. You're *mine*, Shep."

The helicopter doors opened. She watched the medical team lift Shep off the aircraft. Ren leaped out, then turned to help her out. She wanted to get to sick bay. She wanted to be there when he woke up, no matter how long that took.

She marched across the deck, following the medical team.

"Ms. Sinclair?"

She turned her head and saw two men and a woman, all of them wearing suits.

"We're with the Secret Service," the older of the two men said. "I'm Agent Hill. Your father sent us to bring you home. We have a helicopter ready to take us to CSL Comalapa in El Salvador. There'll be a jet waiting to fly you home to your father. He's eager to see you."

Hayden blinked, trying to get her brain firing. She knew a CSL was a cooperative security location, essentially a US base in another country. She shook her head. "I'm sorry, Agent Hill, but I'm not leaving. Shep's been shot. The man who rescued me. He's going into surgery, and I'm staying."

Agent Hill reached out and took her arm. "I'm sure once we're in the air, we can get an update if the operator survives surgery."

If? She made a choked sound and wrenched her arm free. "He's going to survive. And I'm staying."

The man looked down at her, taking in her blood-stained clothes and hands. "Ms. Sinclair, it's obvious you've been through a terrible ordeal, and aren't thinking clearly."

She stiffened. "I'm thinking just fine, and I'm not the one who got shot."

"I'm sorry." The female agent held up a hand, her tone placating. "Your father's orders are for us to bring you home."

"I said *no.*"

Ren stepped forward. "Look, just leave her alone for now. We can—"

"Stand back." The younger Secret Service agent shouldered in front of Ren, blocking him.

Agent Hill grabbed Hayden's arm again.

She couldn't believe this. "I'm not leaving him!"

"I'm sorry." Agent Hill lifted her off her feet.

"No!" She kicked and struggled. "Put me down!"

The agent started toward another helicopter parked on the deck.

"Put her down," Ren barked from nearby. She heard a scuffle as she kept trying to break Hill's hold on her.

"She's clearly traumatized," the female agent said.

"No, listen to me—"

"Do it," Hill said.

Suddenly, the woman moved in close to Hayden, and she felt a prick on the back of her neck.

"What the hell?" Hayden slapped a hand over her neck. "Leave me alone." She twisted and jerked, and seriously considered biting someone. "What did you do?"

"It's just a sedative," the female agent said.

"*No.* I'm not leaving him. I want Shep. I *need* him..."

She could hear Ren yelling angrily, but the world wavered. Her vision dimmed and she felt like all the energy just drained out of her limbs.

Shep. Everything inside her cried out for him.

Her body felt lax, out of her control. Agent Hill hefted her higher and kept walking.

Then it felt like the world got sucked down a dark drain, and there was nothing at all.

CHAPTER EIGHTEEN

S hep opened his eyes and winced.

Everything hurt.

He'd woken like this too many fucking times—sore, weak, and feeling like shit.

He tried to sit up, but pain exploded in his chest. "*Fuck.*" He bit down on his tongue and dropped back on the pillows.

"You're going to rip your stitches out."

He turned his head. A rumpled Ren was sitting in the chair beside Shep's bed.

Blearily, Shep looked around and deduced he was in sick bay on a military ship. *Shit.* How the hell did he get here? What mission had he and the team been on?

"The doctors worked pretty hard to put you back together," Ren said. "You're pretty damn lucky."

Shep reached up and touched the bandage on his shoulder.

"Gunshot wound to the chest," Ren said cheerily.

Shep grunted. Looked like he was going to have a new scar to add to his collection.

"You really should stop getting shot," Ren suggested.

Shot? Wait, he wasn't Ghost Ops anymore, nor was Ren. Memories flooded in like water from a broken dam.

He'd been shot protecting Hayden.

Hayden.

He glanced around and his chest locked. "Where is she?"

"Back in D.C."

Shep felt his insides twist and go cold. He felt like he had frostbite in his chest.

He leaned his head back on the pillows. "She's okay?"

"Yes, physically she's fine. You saved her."

Shep squeezed his eyes closed. *Thank fuck.* Then he opened them and frowned at Ren. "Physically?"

"Emotionally, not so much. I watched her being carried, kicking and screaming, away by the Secret Service, until they sedated her to get her on the helo."

Shep felt a spurt of anger. Oh, she'd chew someone out for that.

"She didn't want to leave you."

His chest warmed a fraction, but he stomped on it. "Okay."

"Okay?" Ren leaned forward. "That's all you have to say?"

"She's where she's supposed to be."

"You fucking love her, you idiot. You deserve her, and she wants you, you lucky son of a bitch."

"I know someone who wanted you. Someone smart

and beautiful. You ran."

A look crossed Ren's face. "We're not talking about me."

"You wouldn't let yourself have her." Shep shook his head. "I get it, Ren. We've seen shit, done shit, and it's taken chunks out of us and left its scars."

Hayden deserved better. She deserved better than a broken, grumpy ex-soldier. She deserved everything.

"Besides, she doesn't want a man or relationship. She had a slick, lawyer ex who fucked her over, and cheated on her. Neither of us wanted a relationship."

"And things change. Shep—"

"It's for the best, Ren." Shep stared up at the ceiling. He was done talking.

His friend made a frustrated noise, just as a nurse appeared.

"He needs to rest," the woman said.

Shep closed his eyes. What he needed to do was get back to his mountain.

HAYDEN SAT by the large window, watching the dreary D.C. winter day. Rain splattered on the glass. Outside, she saw a White House security guard in a raincoat walking by.

It had been five days without Shep. She closed her eyes. She didn't even know if he was alive.

She had to believe he was. She pressed a palm to her aching chest. She had to believe he was somewhere, being super grumpy, as he recovered.

ANNA HACKETT

She'd been transported back to her father. He'd been relieved and overjoyed to see her, until she'd demanded to go back to Shep.

Her father hadn't listened.

They'd argued. He'd told her she was traumatized. She'd been forced to rest, and to be fair, she'd slept almost twenty hours the first day. Her body had been exhausted, and her heart sick.

She wanted Shep.

Another hard thing had been attending Maria's funeral. Her family was devastated. Hayden watched a huge rain drop roll down the window. Hayden still couldn't believe her friend was gone. She'd laid a bunch of white lilies on Maria's casket—they'd been the Secret Service agent's favorite—and spent a minute thanking her friend. And telling her about the man who'd gotten her out of the jungle.

Maria would have loved Shep.

The door opened. "I have a break from my meetings." Her father walked in, looking handsome in his suit. "I've asked Helen to bring us some tea."

Hayden didn't respond.

Her father sat on the couch across from her. "Sweetheart." His tone was what she'd define as cautious. "It's been suggested you should talk to someone. About your ordeal."

She looked at him. "I'm fine, Dad. I survived. Thanks to Shep. I don't even know if he's okay. He got shot—" she closed her eyes, the pain weighing on her "—protecting me."

"And I'm grateful for his actions."

"I want to see him."

Her father cleared his throat. "He knows where you are, but hasn't reached out."

That stung a little, but she knew her stubborn grump wouldn't reach out.

"These men, their identities are a secret for a reason," her father continued.

"He's not in the military anymore, Dad. Do you at least know if he's okay?"

Her father shook his head.

"Don't you care? He risked his life to get me out of Nicaragua."

"Of course, I care." Her father ran a hand through his hair. "I've just been more focused on you." He reached out and took her hand. "Every second you were a captive, I was terrified. I was worried what they'd do to you, that they'd kill you. I can't lose you, Hayden. I lost your mother—" His voice cracked.

"I'm okay, Dad." She squeezed his hand. "I promise."

"Except for your fixation on this man."

She made an angry sound. "Dad—"

He held up a hand. "I'm sure he was very heroic. But you were in intense and dangerous circumstances together. It's easy to...confuse how you feel."

"His name is Shep. And I know how intense and dangerous it was because I was there. This is not an adrenaline-fueled fantasy. What I feel is *real*."

"You barely know him. You don't even know his surname."

Her belly clenched. Her father liked to remind her of that little nugget every day. "It doesn't matter because I know *him*. The man." She smiled. "He's rough and grumpy as hell."

Her father snorted. "That's not very convincing."

"He's also loyal, protective, a man who does what's right with no thought to himself. From the moment I met him—" she laughed "—okay, I punched him the first time I met him, then we sort of wrestled in the mud."

Her father's eyes widened.

"He was brusque, gruff, annoying, but he never lied to me. He protected me, took care of me. He got me everything I needed. He held me when I cried, even though it made him uncomfortable."

Now her father sighed. "I know what these special forces men are like, Hayden. They're different. Dangerous. I'd always imagined you with someone more polished, articulate, and—"

"Like Dillon?"

Her father winced. "Point taken."

"Dad, you're not a snob. Shep's a little rough around the edges, but he's a good man."

Her father's blue gaze moved over her face, staring at her intently. "You don't really know him."

"I know the important parts, but I want the chance to learn the rest of him. You once told me that you saw Mom across the room at a party and you just knew."

Now her dad smiled. It was that secret smile that her parents had always shared.

"I *know* with Shep." Hayden hadn't wanted a man or a relationship. Until her grumpy hero had arrived in her life. Somehow, he'd become the hero she wanted.

"Jesus." Her father pinched the bridge of his nose.

"Maybe I've just been afraid to lose my little girl, especially when I just got you back."

"You'll never lose me." She moved over and sat beside him. She hugged him hard. Even though he'd been refusing to listen to her, she knew it came from a place of love.

He hugged her back. "I just want you safe."

"I know."

"I'll make some calls. Find your Shep."

"Vander Norcross knows him."

Her father froze and pulled back. "Norcross?"

"They served together."

A grimace crossed her father's face. "Shep was Ghost Ops?"

She nodded.

Her father frowned. "Hayden, Ghost Ops soldiers are…"

"Scary?"

"I was going to say dangerous."

"Shep is dangerous, but not to me."

SHEP'S boots crunched on the snow. He dropped a small log into the burning fire pit. The move tugged at his healing wound, and he winced.

It had been over a week since he'd been shot. The bullet had hit some blood vessels, but he'd been lucky that there hadn't been any damage to his heart and lungs. The wound was healing up fine. He'd always healed quickly—something his team had always given him hell for.

He'd been transported from the USS *Blackburn* back to the US. He'd then discharged himself from the hospital. They'd wanted to keep him longer, but he'd just wanted to go home.

He could heal up just as fine here.

He sat on one of the wooden stumps beside his fire pit and looked up at the mountains. The sun was setting, and he loved this time of day. That moment just as the light was dying, and night was about to fall. They'd had a good amount of snow yesterday, and everything all around—mountains, trees, and his cabins—were covered in white.

Colorless.

Pretty much how he felt.

He scowled. He was *not* thinking of Hayden. He gritted his teeth together and stared at the flames. She was safe and back where she belonged.

Shifting on the stump, his chest throbbed, and he welcomed the pain.

He heard the cabin door slam. He saw Ren making his way over, carrying two steaming mugs in his hands.

"Here."

Shep took the coffee, and also smelled whiskey. As he lifted it, his wound tugged again.

He thought he'd hidden his wince, but his friend scowled at him.

"You haven't taken your pain meds."

"I don't need them."

"Stubborn bastard."

"They mess with my head. I'm fine." Shep sipped the coffee. Oh, yeah. He enjoyed the burn of the whiskey.

Ren leaned back on his log. He'd taken some leave to bring Shep home and make sure he didn't die. He was sleeping on Shep's couch and bullying him about resting.

"You're being stubborn about Hayden too," Ren added.

Shep felt every muscle in his back tense. "She's not up for discussion."

"You're falling for her. You deserve to be happy."

"I did my job. She's safe."

"And you're here, stewing in your own misery."

"It's what I do best." The words came out harshly. Shep shook his head. "She deserves better. Someone without all the ugly baggage."

"Oh? Someone suave and charming, like the ex that you told me about?"

Shep growled. The idea of Hayden with *any* man felt like a knife to the gut.

"You're a good fucking man, Shep. The best. Protective. Always willing to step in, even if you do bitch about it. And you care. Your misplaced guilt about your sister and the guys proves that. It's time to let them go. It's time to stop punishing yourself and live. It's time to believe you deserve happiness and love."

Shep just stared at Ren, his words ricocheting around in his head.

Ren finished his coffee. "Stubborn as always." He rose and headed back into the cabin.

Shep just sat there, staring at the fire, emotions churning inside him.

CHAPTER NINETEEN

Gritting his teeth, Shep leaned under the hood of his truck. "Come on you—"

The wrench slipped, and he whacked his knuckles, and jarred his chest in the process. Pain shot through him.

Muttering a string of curses, he stopped to catch his breath.

All he could think about was Hayden.

Last night after dinner with Ren, he'd laid in bed thinking about her. The way she rolled her eyes, her laugh, the look on her face when he had his mouth on her. He'd jerked off thinking about her.

"Dammit." He closed his eyes. He was never going to stop thinking about her.

Because Ren was right—he was falling in love with her.

She was *his*. He felt that in his bones.

He opened his eyes, barely seeing his dusty barn nor

the glimpse of blue sky and snow-dusted trees out the open barn door.

Fuck it. He set the wrench down. He was going to find his woman.

As he stepped outside, he heard a car engine and frowned. Ren was in the cabin, and hadn't said he was headed out anywhere today. Shep shielded his eyes as he watched a small SUV carefully maneuver up his driveway. Someone wasn't used to driving in the snow.

The vehicle stopped and the driver's side door opened.

The Colorado sun glinted off blonde hair.

He froze.

Hayden stepped out, dressed in fitted jeans, boots, and a white jacket. She scanned the cabins, then her gaze moved toward the barn.

It snagged on him.

He drank her in like a man dying of thirst. He was so starved to capture every detail of her.

Her face hardened and she stomped in his direction.

She looked fucking gorgeous, even when she was pissed.

"Shepherd Barlow." There was fury in her voice. "It took me a while to find you. Of course, you didn't even bother to try and find me."

Shep assumed that Vander had told her where he lived.

She stopped two feet away, her chest heaving. "I didn't know if you were dead or alive." She threw her arms in the air. "Everyone kept telling me I was crazy to want a guy I'd only known for less than a week. A guy I met in dangerous circumstances."

"Maybe they were right?" he said.

Her eyes sparked. "I'd hit you, but I know you're healing from a gunshot wound. And they're *not* right!" Her voice echoed through the clearing. "You know they're not right."

"Yeah, I do."

"Because what we shared was real... Wait, what?" Her brows drew together. "You agree with me?"

He cupped her cheeks. Touching her soft skin again felt so good. "Yes. I was about to come and find you."

Her brown gaze narrowed. "Oh, you were coming to find me *now*, just as I arrived here. Why should I believe you?"

"Because I've never lied to you."

She stilled.

"I've been miserable without you," he continued. "I tried to convince myself that you deserve better."

"I probably do." She sniffed. "But for some unknown reason, I'm falling in love with you, Shepherd Barlow."

Fuck. He liked hearing that. Those words arrowed straight to his chest. "Good, because some slick guy in a suit can't have you."

She shot him a confused look as he pulled her into his arms. He took a deep breath, pulling in her scent.

She settled her hands on his shoulders. "I bet you'd look good in a suit."

"I hate suits."

She laughed. "Of course, you do." Her hands moved

to cup his cheeks. "And you're the man I deserve, Shep. A good, honest, protective man."

Shep kissed her. Their tongues tangled and he kissed her deep and long. She moaned into his mouth, and he tilted his head, going deeper. God, he'd missed her silken mouth.

They kissed and kissed, neither wanting to stop.

When they finally came up for air, he pressed his cheek against hers. "I missed you."

She made a sound. "I missed you, too, but I'm still mad at you."

He rubbed his nose against hers. "I know. I'll make it up to you. And I'm falling for you too, Hayden. You've gotten under my skin. You've made me feel. Feel things I didn't want to feel."

Her lovely face softened. "I'll make sure you never regret it."

"I fought it. But you were just too beautiful, smart, courageous—"

This time she kissed him, going up on her toes. She kissed his mouth, then sank her teeth into his bottom lip. "I'm not so mad now. I love it when you use your words."

He growled. "Smartass."

"Grump." She nibbled at his lip. "But you're my grump."

Then Shep shut her up by closing his mouth over hers.

A low chuckle made them pull apart, both of them breathing heavily. They both looked over at Ren, who looked very amused.

"Hayden, nice to see you."

"Ren? What are you doing here?"

"Someone had to keep an eye on the big guy while he healed up, and nursed his broken heart."

Shep growled.

"Took you long enough." Ren turned. "I just made a fresh pot of coffee. Come in when you're finished making out."

HAYDEN THREW her head back and moaned.

They were in Shep's big wooden bed. Due to his injury, she got to be on top. He was sitting on the bed with his back against the headboard, propped up on pillows.

She was riding his big cock.

"*Fuck*, Hayden." He gripped her hips as she rode him. His eyes glittered, locked on her.

She lifted up, then sank back down. *God.* She bit her lip, enjoying the feel of him stretching her, filling her, connecting them.

She leaned forward and kissed him, sliding her hands into his hair.

"You feel so good." His voice was a deep growl. He tugged her closer, cupped one of her breasts, then closed his mouth over her nipple.

She scraped her nails over his scalp, then down the sides of his neck. She rocked against him. The glide of his cock was driving her crazy.

"You fit me perfectly." He switched to her other breast. "My perfect Hayden."

"*Shep.*" Her voice was husky, and the pleasure made it hard to think. She kept riding him, plunging her hips up and down.

"Get there, princess."

She panted, grinding down on him. Then he slid a hand down her belly and found her clit. He rolled it between his fingers, and she cried out. She felt her orgasm growing, larger and larger.

"This is right where I need to be," he said with a grunt. "My cock buried deep inside you, feeling your pussy gripping me."

God, she loved it when he talked like that. When he shared the raw truth of what he wanted, what he liked.

"I'm close," she breathed.

"Good. You going to milk me dry, make me come so hard I can't see anything but you?"

She moaned his name, balanced on the edge.

"Come, princess."

She did. She screamed his name, her back arching.

Her climax triggered his. As she drowned in her pleasure, she watched his rugged face as he found his.

Both breathing heavily, she dropped forward onto his uninjured side, resting her face on his broad shoulder. They lay there, her body still humming as she noted the rise and fall of his chest, the warmth of his skin, the male smell of him.

One of his hands slid up her back. She loved the way he touched her. She could feel the possession in his caress, and she loved how much he wanted her.

"Shit, I can still feel your pussy squeezing my cock." His hand moved down and cupped her ass.

"I hope we didn't make too much noise." She was conscious that Ren was around. She was so touched that he'd come back with Shep to watch over him while he recuperated.

They'd all had dinner together after she'd arrived. Ren hadn't hidden how glad he was that she'd come.

"He went out," Shep said. "He said he was going to a bar in town for a bit."

To give them some alone time. He was a good friend.

She sat back, her gaze falling to the white bandage on his chest. She gently traced the edges of it. She'd come so close to losing him.

"So, are we official now?" As she spoke, she wondered why she felt a flash of nerves.

Shep's gaze moved to her face. "Official?"

She huffed. "A couple, Shep. I know it's a foreign concept for you, but it means you and me, together."

He shifted her off him and Hayden felt a horrible clutch in her chest.

He rose, and for a second, she was distracted by his muscular ass. As he pulled on jeans, she frowned at him. Then he slipped his fleece-lined suede jacket over his bare chest. She didn't miss his wince as he slipped his arm into the sleeve on his injured side.

"Shep?" Her stomach tumbled around a few times. "If this topic is—"

Without warning, he scooped her up into his arms.

She yelped. "You're going to hurt yourself!"

"I'm fine, as long as you don't wriggle."

She went still.

One handed, he snatched a woolen blanket off the bed and wrapped her in it.

"Shep, what are—?"

"Shh."

He carried her through the living room, paused at the front door to slip into his boots, and then he was out the door.

The cold night air nipped at her exposed skin. Shep held her tight, walking across the snow. That's when she spied the glow of the fire pit.

"I asked Ren to start it earlier." Shep sat down on a wooden stump and settled her on his lap.

She snuggled into him. "A fire pit in the snow. This is nice."

"Look up."

She tilted her head back and saw the beautiful stars littering the night sky overhead. Like dozens of jewels spread out to admire. "Beautiful."

"The stars have nothing on you."

She looked at him. "Look at you with the charm."

"It's the truth." He ran a finger along her jaw. "And yes, we're a couple."

Warmth suffused her. He didn't use a lot of words, but when he did, he picked the right ones. "Are you going to ask me to go steady?" she teased.

"No."

She raised her eyebrows.

"We're getting married."

Of their own accord, Hayden's eyes went wide. "What?"

"You're mine. I'm yours. I want the world to know it."

He gripped her chin. "I want to claim you in every way I know how."

She blinked. "Wow." Her throat was thick. "What happened to the grumpy, no-relationship Shep Barlow?"

"He fell in love."

Hayden felt like she was melting.

"And I know you told me that you don't ever want to get married—"

"I think I've changed my mind," she whispered. She cupped his bearded cheek. "Because I'm falling right back in love with you." She touched her mouth to his. "And I'll marry you, Shep. But only after you find a beautiful ring and propose properly."

His lips curled. "You're going to make me go to a jewelry store."

"I'm sure the big, tough former Ghost Ops soldier can survive it."

He nodded. "I can do that."

"Good." Then she kissed her grumpy hero under the stars.

CHAPTER TWENTY

Through the window of the cabin, Ren watched Shep and Hayden outside in the snow. Hayden was skipping along, a smile on her face. She wore a blue woolen hat topped with a ridiculous red pompom.

She looked happy.

Hell, Shep was smiling, too.

Something Ren hadn't seen his friend do much, especially not in the last few years.

As he watched, Hayden crouched, then sprung up and threw a snowball at Shep. It exploded all over his chest.

With a fake roar, he charged, lifting her off her feet. Her laughter filled the air. Then Shep was kissing her.

Shep Barlow in love. Ren shook his head. It was a hell of a thing.

He'd never thought he'd see it. Never thought Shep would let it happen.

But he had. The man deserved it. Deserved a woman like Hayden, and all the love and happiness she'd bring him. Ren was pretty sure that Hayden would smooth out some of Shep's battered edges.

Shep set Hayden down. She looked up at him, and the look on her face made Ren's chest tighten. It was so intimate. Something he shouldn't see.

What would it be like to have a woman look at him like that?

Ren turned away. There was only one woman he wanted to see looking at him like that, and she was off-limits.

Yeah, the daughter of his best friend and mentor was definitely not for him. It was a line he'd never cross.

He finished packing his duffel bag.

Shep was on the mend and no longer alone. Ren had received a message today, and he needed to get back to his ship.

He slung his bag over his shoulder and headed out of the cabin.

The happy couple turned. Hayden frowned, dusting the snow off her gloves. "You're leaving?"

"I need to get back to my ship. I have a big research job coming up. A favor for a friend." He looked at Shep. "For Tom."

Shep nodded.

"And now I know that my guy here will be well looked after, I can go."

Shep scowled. "I can look after myself."

Hayden winked. "I've got him."

"I know you do." Ren leaned down to kiss her, then bent her back over his arm dramatically.

She laughed, and Shep crossed his arms over his chest and scowled.

Ren set her back on her feet, then looked at his friend. "Be happy, you stubborn asshole."

Shaking his head, Shep reached out and hugged Ren hard. "Be careful."

"You know me." Ren smiled. "I'm always careful."

"No, you're always getting into trouble."

Shep walked Ren over to his rental car.

"Take care of your woman, Shep."

"I will. She's worth everything, Ren. Worth every risk, every worry, everything."

Ren smiled. "I'm happy for you."

Shep lowered his voice. "Take the risk, Ren."

Ren stiffened.

"You deserve some love and happiness too," Shep added.

"The ocean is the only lady I need."

"No, she's not."

Ren just ignored his friend, slapped Shep on the back, then slid into his vehicle.

"Now who's the stubborn asshole," Shep muttered.

Ren started the engine. He wasn't being stubborn, he just knew better than anyone that you didn't always get the things you wanted.

A few weeks later

SHEP FINISHED up work on his truck for the day and wiped his hands on a rag. The Chevy was coming along nicely. He should have the engine fully rebuilt soon.

He felt a vibration in his pocket and pulled out his cellphone. He saw Vander's name and smiled.

He pressed the phone to his ear. "Norcross."

"How's the bullet wound?" Vander asked.

"Healing up nicely."

"You always did heal quickly. And how's Hayden?"

"She's good."

"Just checking you hadn't scared her off."

Shep leaned against his truck. "For some reason, she loves me."

"You're a lucky man." Vander paused. "I guess this is the point where I tell you I told you so."

Shep smiled. "Fuck off."

"You should be thanking me. I told you that you needed to quit hiding and—"

"Fine, fine. You can quit rubbing it in."

Vander's low laugh came across the line.

"Vander," Shep pulled in a breath, "thank you."

"I've always got your back, Shep."

When Shep finished talking with Vander—and made a promise that he and Hayden would visit San Francisco when they could—he headed out of the barn. It was time to find his woman.

He smiled. Claiming Hayden as his had turned out to be the easiest thing he'd ever done. They'd slipped into life together without too many bumps.

Oh, they still argued. His smile widened. They both

enjoyed it, although he enjoyed making up afterward the most.

They cooked together, did some snowshoeing, and she helped him in the barn. She'd taken leave from her work, but he knew she'd been making calls to universities in Denver to find research work closer to home.

She said she loved the idea of living in Colorado, and had no desire to go back to Washington D.C. She was already planning hikes, and visits to all the local National Parks for the springtime.

There was no sign of her getting bored of Colorado or him.

He headed into the cabin, and toed off his boots. He heard her on the phone. She was sitting on a stool at the kitchen counter, her back to him.

"That sounds great. *So* great. Thank you, Professor Ward." She did a little fist pump in the air. "I'm really looking forward to it."

As she ended the call, Shep slid his arms around her from behind. Now that his wound was healed up, he barely felt a twinge in his chest.

"*Shep.*" She jolted. "I always forget how quietly you move."

He kissed the side of her neck. "Who was on the phone?"

She spun in his arms, a huge smile on her face. "My new boss."

Shep raised a brow.

"Professor Oliver Ward at DU. I joined his team." She clapped her hands together. "He's a legend. And his wife is rather notorious. She's a treasure hunter." Hayden's eyes gleamed.

"I've heard of them."

Her brow creased. "You have?"

"I know their kids. Declan runs—"

"Treasure Hunter Security."

Shep nodded. "That firefight we had here when Boone's girlfriend Gemma was in danger, the Treasure Hunter Security team helped out."

Hayden blinked. "Really?"

"Really. So, you're going to work in Denver?"

"I won't need to go in all the time. It'll depend on the projects." Then she fidgeted. "But Professor Ward does need my help in the field first. Not in Central America, thankfully."

"Good." Because there was no chance in hell Shep was letting her go to Central America.

"It's an Ancestral Puebloan project." Passion and energy radiated off her. "At Mesa Verde National Park. They found some undiscovered ruins in a cave. It could be the next Cliff Palace." She pulled her face. "It's not too far away, but I would be gone for a bit."

Shep wrapped an arm around her. "It's fine. I'm coming too."

"What? No, Shep, you'd be bored. It—"

"No, I won't be bored because I'm the new head of security for the dig."

"What?" she breathed.

"I spoke to Oliver about it earlier."

She smacked his arm. "You sneak." She grinned. "I'm so damn happy."

"Me too." He wrapped his arms around her. "Every time I look at you."

She snuggled into him. "I think this calls for a special dinner tonight. Steaks, baked potatoes, and beer."

Shep knew that Jenny would love Hayden. And Miles, Charlie, and Julio would be giving him a thumbs up.

For the first time in his life, he felt something he thought might be true contentment.

That's when he heard an engine.

Scratch that, engines plural.

He frowned. "We have visitors."

"Expecting anyone?" she asked.

"No."

They stepped outside to see three black SUVs pull up in front of the cabins. They had government plates, and Shep's shoulders tensed.

The vehicles pulled to a stop and lots of doors opened. Several people in suits got out, scanning around.

Then a familiar man with a regal face and salt-and-pepper hair stepped out of the back of the middle SUV.

Oh, shit.

The President of the United States had arrived for a visit.

The man whose daughter Shep was fucking.

"Crap," he muttered.

Hayden elbowed him. "You're a brave military hero, remember?"

"Right now, I'm just a man who dared to touch his daughter."

She snorted. "I love you."

Her father walked over to them, and Hayden moved to meet him.

"Dad." She hugged him.

"Hello, sweetheart." The president looked over her head and met Shep's gaze.

Shep held out a hand. "Shep Barlow, sir."

"Aaron Sinclair." He took Shep's hand and shook it. "So, you're the one who rescued my girl."

"She likes to tell me that she rescued herself."

Hayden pulled a face.

Her father smiled. "That sounds like her."

Hayden put her hands on her hips. "Hello, I'm standing right here."

"She looks happy," Aaron Sinclair said.

"I do my best every day to keep her that way." Shep nodded a head toward the cabin. "Coffee? You can tell me more about Hayden. Maybe about when she was younger."

"I have lots of stories, Shep. Can I call you Shep?"

"Absolutely."

Hayden groaned. "How long are you staying, Dad?"

"I cleared a couple of days. Everyone thinks I'm at Camp David." He scanned around, taking in the cabins. "Looks like you guys have room here."

Shit, the president was going to be staying at his place. Shep nodded. "More than enough room."

Aaron Sinclair smiled. "Excellent."

Shep slung an arm around Hayden, and she slipped an arm around his waist. Then she smiled up at him.

That smile. He'd do a lot of things to see that smile.

Yes, this woman was everything to him.

He'd face the jungle, deadly abductors, bullets, explosions, and having the president as a future father-in-law, as long as Hayden was his.

Shep led his woman inside to have coffee with her father.

I hope you enjoyed Shep and Hayden's story!

Unbroken Heroes continues with *The Hero She Craves*, starring charming loner Ren Santoro. Coming June 2024.

If you'd like to know more about **Declan Ward** (and his father Oliver) and the Treasure Hunter Security team, then check out the Treasure Hunter Security series, starting with *Undiscovered*.

If you'd like to know more about **Vander Norcross** and his team, then check out the first Norcross Security book, *The Investigator*. **Read on for a preview of the first chapter.**

Don't miss out! For updates about new releases, free books, and other fun stuff, sign up for my VIP mailing list and get your *free box set* containing three action-packed romances.

Visit here to get started: www.annahackett.com

Would you like a FREE BOX SET of my books?

PREVIEW: THE INVESTIGATOR

There was a glass of chardonnay with her name on it waiting for her at home.

Haven McKinney smiled. The museum was closed, and she was *done* for the day.

As she walked across the East gallery of the Hutton Museum, her heels clicked on the marble floor.

God, she loved the place. The creamy marble that made up the flooring and wrapped around the grand pillars was gorgeous. It had that hushed air of grandeur that made her heart squeeze a little every time she stepped inside. But more than that, the amazing art the Hutton housed sang to the art lover in her blood.

Snagging a job here as the curator six months ago had been a dream come true. She'd been at a low point in her life. Very low. Haven swallowed a snort and circled a stunning white-marble sculpture of a naked, reclining woman with the most perfect resting bitch face. She'd never guessed that her life would come crashing down at age twenty-nine.

She lifted her chin. Miami was her past. The Hutton and San Francisco were her future. No more throwing caution to the wind. She had a plan, and she was sticking to it.

She paused in front of a stunning exhibit of traditional Chinese painting and calligraphy. It was one of their newer exhibits, and had been Haven's brainchild. Nearby, an interactive display was partially assembled. Over the next few days, her staff would finish the installation. Excitement zipped through Haven. She couldn't wait to have the touchscreens operational. It was her passion to make art more accessible, especially to children. To help them be a part of it, not just look at it. To learn, to feel, to enjoy.

Art had helped her through some of the toughest times in her life, and she wanted to share that with others.

She looked at the gorgeous old paintings again. One portrayed a mountainous landscape with beautiful maple trees. It soothed her nerves.

Wine would soothe her nerves, as well. *Right*. She

needed to get upstairs to her office and grab her handbag, then get an Uber home.

Her cell phone rang and she unclipped it from the lanyard she wore at the museum. "Hello?"

"Change of plans, girlfriend," a smoky female voice said. "Let's go out and celebrate being gorgeous, successful, and single. I'm done at the office, and believe me, it has been a *grueling* day."

Haven smiled at her new best friend. She'd met Gia Norcross when she joined the Hutton. Gia's wealthy brother, Easton Norcross, owned the museum, and was Haven's boss. The museum was just a small asset in the businessman's empire. Haven suspected Easton owned at least a third of San Francisco. Maybe half.

She liked and respected her boss. Easton could be tough, but he valued her opinions. And she loved his bossy, take-charge, energetic sister. Gia ran a highly successful PR firm in the city, and did all the PR and advertising for the Hutton. They'd met not long after Haven had started work at the museum.

After their first meeting, Gia had dragged Haven out to her favorite restaurant and bar, and the rest was history.

"I guess making people's Instagram look pretty and not staged is hard work," Haven said with a grin.

"Bitch." Gia laughed. "God, I had a meeting with a businessman caught in...well, let's just say he and his assistant were *not* taking notes on the boardroom table."

Haven felt an old, unwelcome memory rise up. She mentally stomped it down. "I don't feel sorry for the cheating asshole, I feel sorry for whatever poor shmuck got more than they were paid for when they walked into the boardroom."

"Actually, it was the cheating businessman's wife."

"Uh-oh."

"And the assistant was male," Gia added.

"Double uh-oh."

"Then said cheater comes to my PR firm, telling me to clean up his mess, because he's thinking he might run for governor one day. I mean, I'm good, but I can't wrangle miracles."

Haven suspected that Gia had verbally eviscerated the man and sent him on his way. Gia Norcross had a sharp tongue, and wasn't afraid to use it.

"So, grueling day and I need alcohol. I'll meet you at ONE65, and the first drink is on me."

"I'm pretty wiped, Gia—"

"Uh-uh, no excuses. I'll see you in an hour." And with that, Gia was gone.

Haven clipped her phone to her lanyard. Well, it looked like she was having that chardonnay at ONE65, the six-story, French dining experience Gia loved. Each level offered something different, from patisserie, to bistro and grill, to bar and lounge.

Haven walked into the museum's main gallery, and her blood pressure dropped to a more normal level. It was her favorite space in the museum. The smell of wood, the gorgeous lights gleaming overhead, and the amazing paintings combined to create a soothing room. She smoothed her hands down her fitted, black skirt. Haven was tall, at five foot eight, and curvy, just like her mom had been. Her boobs, currently covered by a cute, white blouse with a tie around her neck, weren't much to write home about, but she had to buy her skirts one size bigger. She sighed. No matter how much she walked or jogged —*blergh*, okay, she didn't jog much—she still had an ass.

Even in her last couple of months in Miami, when stress had caused her to lose a bunch of weight due to everything going on, her ass hadn't budged.

Memories of Miami—and her douchebag-of-epic-proportions-ex—threatened, churning like storm clouds on the horizon.

Nope. She locked those thoughts down. She was *not* going there.

She had a plan, and the number one thing for taking back and rebuilding her life was *no* men. She'd sworn off anyone with a Y chromosome.

She didn't need one, didn't want one, she was D-O-N-E, done.

She stopped in front of the museum's star attraction. Claude Monet's *Water Lilies*.

Haven loved the impressionist's work. She loved the colors, the delicate strokes. This one depicted water lilies and lily pads floating on a gentle pond. His paintings always made an impact, and had a haunting, yet soothing feel to them.

It was also worth just over a hundred million dollars.

The price tag still made her heart flutter. She'd put a business case to Easton, and they'd purchased the painting three weeks ago at auction. Haven had planned out the display down to the rivets used on the wood. She'd thrown herself into the project.

Gia had put together a killer marketing campaign,

and Haven had reluctantly been interviewed by the local paper. But it had paid off. Ticket sales to the museum were up, and everyone wanted to see *Water Lilies*.

Footsteps echoed through the empty museum, and she turned to see a uniformed security guard appear in the doorway.

"Ms. McKinney?"

"Yes, David? I was just getting ready to leave."

"Sorry to delay you. There's a delivery truck at the back entrance. They say they have a delivery of a Zadkine bronze."

Haven frowned, running through the next day's schedule in her head. "That's due tomorrow."

"It sounds like they had some other deliveries nearby and thought they'd squeeze it in."

She glanced at her slim, silver wristwatch, fighting back annoyance. She'd had a long day, and now she'd be late to meet Gia. "Fine. Have them bring it in."

With a nod, David disappeared. Haven pulled out her phone and quickly fired off a text to warn Gia that she'd be late. Then Haven headed up to her office, and checked her notes for tomorrow. She had several calls to make to chase down some pieces for a new exhibit she wanted to launch in the winter. There were some restoration quotes to go over, and a charity gala for her art charity to plan. She needed to get down into the storage rooms and see if there was anything they could cycle out and put on display.

God, she loved her job. Not many people would get excited about digging around in dusty storage rooms, but Haven couldn't wait.

She made sure her laptop was off and grabbed her handbag. She slipped her lanyard off and stuffed her phone in her bag.

When she reached the bottom of the stairs, she heard a strange noise from the gallery. A muffled pop, then a thump.

Frowning, she took one step toward the gallery.

Suddenly, David staggered through the doorway, a splotch of red on his shirt.

Haven's pulse spiked. *Oh God, was that blood?* "David—"

"Run." He collapsed to the floor.

Fear choking her, she kicked off her heels and spun. She had to get help.

But she'd only taken two steps when a hand sank into her hair, pulling her neat twist loose, and sending her brown hair cascading over her shoulders.

"Let me go!"

She was dragged into the main gallery, and when she lifted her head, her gut churned.

Five men dressed in black, all wearing balaclavas, stood in a small group.

No...oh, no.

Their other guard, Gus, stood with his hands in the air. He was older, former military. She was shoved closer toward him.

"Ms. McKinney, you okay?" Gus asked.

She managed a nod. "They shot David."

"I kn—"

"No talking," one man growled.

Haven lifted her chin. "What do you want?" There was a slight quaver in her voice.

The man who'd grabbed her glared. His cold, blue eyes glittered through the slits in his balaclava. Then he ignored her, and with the others, they turned to face the *Water Lilies*.

Haven's stomach dropped. *No.* This couldn't be happening.

A thin man moved forward, studying the painting's gilt frame with gloved hands. "It's wired to an alarm."

Blue Eyes, clearly the group's leader, turned and aimed the gun at Gus' barrel chest. "Disconnect it."

"No," the guard said belligerently.

"I'm not asking."

Haven held up her hands. "Please—"

The gun fired. Gus dropped to one knee, pressing a hand to his shoulder.

"No!" she cried.

The leader stepped forward and pressed the gun to the older man's head.

"No." Haven fought back her fear and panic. "Don't hurt him. I'll disconnect it."

Slowly, she inched toward the painting, carefully avoiding the thin man still standing close to it. She touched the security panel built in beside the frame, pressing her palm to the small pad.

A second later, there was a discreet beep.

Two other men came forward and grabbed the frame.

She glanced around at them. "You're making a mistake. If you know who owns this museum, then you know you won't get away with this." Who would go up against the Norcross family? Easton, rich as sin, had a lot of connections, but his brother, Vander... Haven suppressed a shiver. Gia's middle brother might be hot, but he scared the bejesus out of Haven.

Vander Norcross, former military badass, owned Norcross Security and Investigations. His team had put in the high-tech security for the museum.

No one in their right mind wanted to go up against Vander, or the third Norcross brother who also worked with Vander, or the rest of Vander's team of badasses.

"Look, if you just—"

The blow to her head made her stagger. She blinked, pain radiating through her face. Blue Eyes had back-handed her.

He moved in and hit her again, and Haven cried out, clutching her face. It wasn't the first time she'd been hit. Her douchebag ex had hit her once. That was the day she'd left him for good.

But this was worse. Way worse.

"Shut up, you stupid bitch."

The next blow sent her to the floor. She thought she heard someone chuckle. He followed with a kick to her ribs, and Haven curled into a ball, a sob in her throat.

Her vision wavered and she blinked. Blue Eyes crouched down, putting his hand to the tiles right in front of her. Dizziness hit her, and she vaguely took in the freckles on the man's hand. They formed a spiral pattern.

"No one talks back to me," the man growled. "Especially a woman." He moved away.

She saw the men were busy maneuvering the painting off the wall. It was easy for two people to move.

She knew its exact dimensions—eighty by one hundred centimeters.

No one was paying any attention to her. Fighting through the nausea and dizziness, she dragged herself a few inches across the floor, closer to the nearby pillar. A pillar that had one of several hidden, high-tech panic buttons built into it.

When the men were turned away, she reached up and pressed the button.

Then blackness sucked her under.

HAVEN SAT on one of the lovely wooden benches she'd had installed around the museum. She'd wanted somewhere for guests to sit and take in the art.

She'd never expected to be sitting on one, holding a melting ice pack to her throbbing face, and staring at the empty wall where a multi-million-dollar masterpiece should be hanging. And she definitely didn't expect to be doing it with police dusting black powder all over the museum's walls.

Tears pricked her eyes. She was alive, her guards were hurt but alive, and that was what mattered. The police had questioned her and she'd told them everything she could remember. The paramedics had checked her over and given her the ice pack. Nothing was broken, but she'd been told to expect swelling and bruising.

David and Gus had been taken to the hospital. She'd been assured the men would be okay. Last she'd heard, David was in surgery. Her throat tightened. *Oh, God.*

What was she going to tell Easton?

Haven bit her lip and a tear fell down her cheek. She hadn't cried in months. She'd shed more than enough tears over Leo after he'd gone crazy and hit her. She'd left Miami the next day. She'd needed to get away from her ex and, unfortunately, despite loving her job at a classy Miami art gallery, Leo's cousin had owned it. Alyssa had been the one who had introduced them.

Haven had learned a painful lesson to not mix business and pleasure.

She'd been done with Leo's growing moodiness, outbursts, and cheating on her and hitting her had been the last straw. *Asshole.*

She wiped the tear away. San Francisco was as far from Miami as she could get and still be in the continental US. This was supposed to be her fresh new start.

She heard footsteps—solid, quick, and purposeful. Easton strode in.

He was a tall man, with dark hair that curled at the collar of his perfectly fitted suit. Haven had sworn off men, but she was still woman enough to appreciate her boss' good looks. His mother was Italian-American, and she'd passed down her very good genes to her children.

Like his brothers, Easton had been in the military, too, although he'd joined the Army Rangers. It showed in his muscled body. Once, she'd seen his shirt sleeves rolled up when they'd had a late meeting. He had some interesting ink that was totally at odds with his sophisticated-businessman persona.

His gaze swept the room, his jaw tight. It settled on her and he strode over.

"Haven—"

"Oh God, Easton. I'm so sorry."

He sat beside her and took her free hand. He squeezed her cold fingers, then he looked at her face and cursed.

She hadn't been brave enough to look in the mirror, but she guessed it was bad.

"They took the *Water Lilies*," she said.

"Okay, don't worry about it just now."

She gave a hiccupping laugh. "Don't worry? It's worth a hundred and ten *million* dollars."

A muscle ticked in his jaw. "You're okay, and that's the main thing. And the guards are in serious but stable condition at the hospital."

She nodded numbly. "It's all my fault."

Easton's gaze went to the police, and then moved back to her. "That's not true."

"I let them in." Her voice broke. God, she wanted the marble floor to crack and swallow her.

"Don't worry." Easton's face turned very serious. "Vander and Rhys will find the painting."

Her boss' tone made her shiver. Something made her suspect that Easton wanted his brothers to find the men who'd stolen the painting more than recovering the price-less piece of art.

She licked her lips, and felt the skin on her cheek tug. She'd have some spectacular bruises later. *Great. Thanks, universe.*

Then Easton's head jerked up, and Haven followed his gaze.

A man stood in the doorway. She hadn't heard him

coming. Nope, Vander Norcross moved silently, like a ghost.

He was a few inches over six feet, had a powerful body, and radiated authority. His suit didn't do much to tone down the sense that a predator had stalked into the room. While Easton was handsome, Vander wasn't. His face was too rugged, and while both he and Easton had blue eyes, Vander's were dark indigo, and as cold as the deepest ocean depths.

He didn't look happy. She fought back a shiver.

Then another man stepped up beside Vander.

Haven's chest locked. *Oh, no. No, no, no.*

She should have known. He was Vander's top investigator. Rhys Matteo Norcross, the youngest of the Norcross brothers.

At first glance, he looked like his brothers—similar build, muscular body, dark hair and bronze skin. But Rhys was the youngest, and he had a charming edge his brothers didn't share. He smiled more frequently, and his shaggy, thick hair always made her imagine him as a rock star, holding a guitar and making girls scream.

Haven was also totally, one hundred percent in lust with him. Any time he got near, he made her body flare to life, her heart beat faster, and made her brain freeze up. She could barely talk around the man.

She did *not* want Rhys Norcross to notice her. Or talk to her. Or turn his soulful, brown eyes her way.

Nuh-uh. No way. She'd sworn off men. This one should have a giant warning sign hanging on him. *Watch out, heartbreak waiting to happen.*

Rhys had been in the military with Vander. Some

hush-hush special unit that no one talked about. Now he worked at Norcross Security—apparently finding anything and anyone.

He also raced cars and boats in his free time. The man liked to go fast. Oh, and he bedded women. His reputation was legendary. Rhys liked a variety of adventures and experiences.

It was lucky Haven had sworn off men.

Especially when they happened to be her boss' brother.

And especially, especially when they were also her best friend's brother.

Off limits.

She saw the pair turn to look her and Easton's way.

Crap. Pulse racing, she looked at her bare feet and red toenails, which made her realize she hadn't recovered her shoes yet. They were her favorites.

She felt the men looking at her, and like she was drawn by a magnet, she looked up. Vander was scowling. Rhys' dark gaze was locked on her.

Haven's traitorous heart did a little tango in her chest.

Before she knew what was happening, Rhys went down on one knee in front of her.

She saw rage twist his handsome features. Then he shocked her by cupping her jaw, and pushing the ice pack away.

They'd never talked much. At Gia's parties, Haven purposely avoided him. He'd never touched her before, and she felt the warmth of him singe through her.

His eyes flashed. "It's going to be okay, baby."

Baby?

He stroked her cheekbone, those long fingers gentle.

Fighting for some control, Haven closed her hand over his wrist. She swallowed. "I—"

"Don't worry, Haven. I'm going to find the man who did this to you and make him regret it."

Her belly tightened. *Oh, God.* When was the last time anyone had looked out for her like this? She was certain no one had ever promised to hunt anyone down for her. Her gaze dropped to his lips.

He had amazingly shaped lips, a little fuller than such a tough man should have, framed by dark stubble.

There was a shift in his eyes and his face warmed. His fingers kept stroking her skin and she felt that caress all over.

Then she heard the click of heels moving at speed. Gia burst into the room.

"What the hell is going on?"

Haven jerked back from Rhys and his hypnotic touch. Damn, she'd been proven right—she was so weak where this man was concerned.

Gia hurried toward them. She was five-foot-four, with a curvy, little body, and a mass of dark, curly hair. As usual, she wore one of her power suits—short skirt, fitted jacket, and sky-high heels.

"Out of my way." Gia shouldered Rhys aside. When her friend got a look at Haven, her mouth twisted. "I'm going to *kill* them."

"Gia," Vander said. "The place is filled with cops. Maybe keep your plans for murder and vengeance quiet."

"Fix this." She pointed at Vander's chest, then at

Rhys. Then she turned and hugged Haven. "You're coming home with me."

"Gia—"

"No. No arguments." Gia held up her palm like a traffic cop. Haven had seen "the hand" before. It was pointless arguing.

Besides, she realized she didn't want to be alone. And the quicker she got away from Rhys' dark, far-too-perceptive gaze, the better.

Norcross Security

The Investigator
The Troubleshooter
The Specialist
The Bodyguard
The Hacker
The Powerbroker
The Detective
The Medic
The Protector
Also Available as Audiobooks!

PREVIEW: TREASURE HUNTER SECURITY

Want to learn more about *Treasure Hunter Security*? Check out the first book in the series, *Undiscovered*, Declan Ward's action-packed story.

One former Navy SEAL. One dedicated

archeologist. One secret map to a fabulous lost oasis.

Finding undiscovered treasures is always daring, dangerous, and deadly. Perfect for the men of Treasure Hunter Security. Former Navy SEAL Declan Ward is haunted by the demons of his past and throws everything he has into his security business—Treasure Hunter Security. Dangerous archeological digs – no problem. Daring expeditions – sure thing. Museum security for invaluable exhibits – easy. But on a simple dig in the Egyptian desert, he collides with a stubborn, smart archeologist, Dr. Layne Rush, and together they get swept into a deadly treasure hunt for a mythical lost oasis. When an evil from his past reappears, Declan vows to do anything to protect Layne.

Dr. Layne Rush is dedicated to building a successful career—a promise to the parents she lost far too young. But when her dig is plagued by strange accidents, targeted by a lethal black market antiquities ring, and artifacts are stolen, she is forced to turn to Treasure Hunter Security, and to the tough, sexy, and too-used-to-giving-orders Declan. Soon her organized dig morphs into a wild treasure hunt across the desert dunes.

Danger is hunting them every step of the way, and Layne and Declan must find a way to work together...to not only find the treasure but to survive.

Treasure Hunter Security
Undiscovered
Uncharted

Unexplored
Unfathomed
Untraveled
Unmapped
Unidentified
Undetected
Also Available as Audiobooks!

ALSO BY ANNA HACKETT

Fury Brothers

Fury

Keep

Also Available as Audiobooks!

Unbroken Heroes

The Hero She Needs

Sentinel Security

Wolf

Hades

Striker

Steel

Excalibur

Hex

Also Available as Audiobooks!

Norcross Security

The Investigator

The Troubleshooter

The Specialist

The Bodyguard

The Hacker

The Powerbroker

The Detective

The Medic

The Protector

Also Available as Audiobooks!

Billionaire Heists

Stealing from Mr. Rich

Blackmailing Mr. Bossman

Hacking Mr. CEO

Also Available as Audiobooks!

Team 52

Mission: Her Protection

Mission: Her Rescue

Mission: Her Security

Mission: Her Defense

Mission: Her Safety

Mission: Her Freedom

Mission: Her Shield

Mission: Her Justice

Also Available as Audiobooks!

Treasure Hunter Security

Undiscovered

Uncharted

Unexplored

Unfathomed

Untraveled

Unmapped

Unidentified

Undetected

Also Available as Audiobooks!

Oronis Knights

Knightmaster

Knighthunter

Galactic Kings

Overlord

Emperor

Captain of the Guard

Conqueror

Also Available as Audiobooks!

Eon Warriors

Edge of Eon

Touch of Eon

Heart of Eon

Kiss of Eon

Mark of Eon

Claim of Eon

Storm of Eon

Soul of Eon

King of Eon

Also Available as Audiobooks!

Galactic Gladiators: House of Rone

Sentinel

Defender

Centurion

Paladin

Guard

Weapons Master

Also Available as Audiobooks!

Galactic Gladiators

Gladiator

Warrior

Hero

Protector

Champion

Barbarian

Beast

Rogue

Guardian

Cyborg

Imperator

Hunter

Also Available as Audiobooks!

Hell Squad

Marcus

Cruz

Gabe

Reed

Roth

Noah

Shaw

Holmes

Niko

Finn

Devlin

Theron

Hemi

Ash

Levi

Manu

Griff

Dom

Survivors

Tane

Also Available as Audiobooks!

The Anomaly Series

Time Thief

Mind Raider

Soul Stealer

Salvation

Anomaly Series Box Set

The Phoenix Adventures

Among Galactic Ruins

At Star's End

In the Devil's Nebula

On a Rogue Planet

Beneath a Trojan Moon

Beyond Galaxy's Edge

On a Cyborg Planet

Return to Dark Earth

On a Barbarian World

Lost in Barbarian Space

Through Uncharted Space

Crashed on an Ice World

Perma Series

Winter Fusion

A Galactic Holiday

Warriors of the Wind

Tempest

Storm & Seduction

Fury & Darkness

Standalone Titles

Savage Dragon

Hunter's Surrender

One Night with the Wolf

For more information visit www.annahackett.com

ABOUT THE AUTHOR

I'm a USA Today bestselling romance author who's passionate about ***fast-paced, emotion-filled*** contemporary romantic suspense and science fiction romance. I love writing about people overcoming unbeatable odds and achieving seemingly impossible goals. I like to believe it's possible for all of us to do the same.

I live in Australia with my own personal hero and two very busy, always-on-the-move sons.

For release dates, behind-the-scenes info, free books, and other fun stuff, sign up for the latest news here:

Website: www.annahackett.com

Made in United States
Orlando, FL
07 February 2024

43393523R00150